THE BIMBOS OF BLOSSOM

A BIMBO TRANSFORMATION NOVEL

SADIE THATCHER

INTRODUCTION

What would happen if an entire town was bimbofied? I created Blossom as a place to find out how it could be done and to have a place where a variety of different characters could experience bimboization.

This novel started as a series of posts on Patreon. They are largely told from the perspective of the bimbofier, whoever they may be. It still reads much like a diary, although there are several chapters that deviate from that general rule.

Unfortunately, the Blossom story was never finished on Patreon. I have revived it here, editing the chapters in a few places, but also finishing the story so the saga of Blossom can finally come to a cohesive end.

Please enjoy this novel about the bimbofication of Blossom, appearing for the first time outside of Patreon and for your reading enjoyment in novel form.

SETTLING IN BLOSSOM

I always put a great deal of thought into the communities I choose to call home. I am sure all people do, at least to a certain extent. But my needs are a little different from most.

You see, I am a bimbofier. When I settle someplace, I do so not because of a job or school. My moves are always with the purpose of spreading the happiness only bimbos can provide.

I have traveled the country and the world, leaving a trail of bimbofied communities behind me. I like to think I leave a place better than when I found it, but I suppose that is up to the observer to decide.

For my next home, I chose Blossom. It is a small island community in the least bimbo place anyone can imagine. It's a small town. People wear flannel. The temperatures are moderated by the nearby cold waters of the sea, making it not too cold, but rarely does it reach bikini weather.

It would have been easy to choose someplace in southern California, or really anywhere in the United States that someone might consider south. But after years of taking the easy route, I decided it is time to take on more of a challenge.

So here I am in Blossom. I'm currently sitting in a little coffee shop, sipping an espresso, that was delivered to me by a flannel and denim wearing barista, while I try to figure out what my first steps will be.

I'm already sensing one problem. The community here is small and tight nit. That will make it harder to enter as an outsider. I will need to find a way to ingratiate myself with the local population, get to know them and let them get to know me. At least let them get to know the part of me that I want them to know. The people here do not need to know everything, like how before I move on, all the women here will be bimbos.

It is hard to keep myself from just making a few beginning changes. The barista should not be wearing such unflattering clothing. I could easily give her a little boost. It would certainly turn her current frown upside down.

But I know I can't tip my hand too early. I need to get the whole town involved before I start making changes. It will need to be large in scale, but slow in action. I can't have someone leave the island for a few days, only to return to a bimbofied population. Alarm bells would ring out and the authorities would be called. While I've never been caught, I have seen others like me face trumped up charges, since while what I do technically isn't a crime, the squares out there in the world don't like it.

I do know one thing. Blossom is perfectly named. Soon everything and everyone will be as beautiful as a blossom.

THE FIRST STEP IN BLOSSOM

I was the newbie in town. I needed a way to get the locals to trust me and make me one of their own. There is a big difference between being a resident of Blossom and being a tourist.

To do that, I needed to open a business in town. Technically, it would not matter what it was, but I wanted to become the go-to hang out location for Blossom residents.

Believe it or not, I got my idea from an airport lounge. You buy a membership or pay a one time fee to get unlimited, or nearly unlimited, access to food and drink, among other services.

However, my "lounge" would have more features and perks. I would also make it free to all residents. Who would pass up free?

I started with buying a warehouse as close to the center of town as I could. I paid a little more for it, but when you have the ability to bimbofy an entire town, you tend not to worry much about money.

I will admit, the renovation took longer than I had hoped. I have learned that Blossom operates on a slightly different time schedule than most other places. The locals call it island time. Delays nearly made me give up on Blossom, but the added challenge resulted in my doubling down on my commitment to bring change to the sleepy little island in the Pacific Northwest.

The hardest part was disguising what the building really was. When it came time to work on the building facade, I felt like I was building a set for a movie. Yes, the building was still a warehouse, but that didn't mean it had to look like one, on the inside and on the outside.

You might question why I chose to use a warehouse as my base, as opposed to another structure. I could have custom built a building to exactly fit my needs or I could have converted an old house or commercial building. What I liked about the warehouse was that it gave me flexibility in the future. Much like a movie set, I could more easily change the arrangement of the different spaces to fit whatever my needs were. But I still named the place Blossom House. I was surprised another business had not adopted it.

It turned out that hiring my contractors from the island was a huge boon to my popularity in town. Things slow down in the off season, fewer tourists visiting and the weather can get a little dreary at times.

I made a big deal out of opening day. Every single Blossom adult resident got an invitation. I pulled out all the stops. A lavish spread of food, a never ending flow of drinks, almost everything locally sourced, were all a part of the draw.

On top of the food and drink, Blossom House offered massages and other spa-like features. There is also a gym, an onsite nutritionist and even counselors for people to get help from.

I made it a point to greet everyone at the door with a big smile and a welcoming gift. I should point out that nothing about the grand opening was untoward. I was not about to start bimbofying the women as soon as they walked in the door. No, that would begin with the second visit. The grand opening was all about making sure there was a second visit.

Of course, I couldn't just leave everything to chance. That special gift everyone received? Just a little something to not just show my thanks for everyone attending the opening, but to help make sure there was a second visit. And a third, a fourth and so forth. I may do things the right way, but that doesn't mean I don't stack the deck in my favor.

In closing, the grand opening was a huge success. Over half the town visited. That means over half the town will soon be under my control. Not that I'm writing everyone else off. They too will find their way into the Blossom House and under my influence. But all that will have to wait.

STARTING THE BIMBO TRANSFORMATION IN BLOSSOM

It felt really good to finally get the actual bimboization started. It really is like a drug for me. My withdrawal symptoms aren't like with street drug addictions, but there are some similarities.

I tried going cold turkey a couple times. Yes, even we bimbofiers have a conscience and sometimes we scare ourselves straight. For me, I could never last. And when I would finally relapse, no one was safe.

The worst was when I bimbofied an entire over 21 movie theater. People walked in with their beers and popcorn and walked out giggling and wondering where they were going to get their next cock from. Incidents like that are hard to keep under the radar. Thankfully, no one ever pointed the finger at me.

But this isn't the story of how I bimbofied a theater full of patrons. This is about how I bimbofied the island town of Blossom.

First, I should take a moment to mention that sometimes I refer to the bimbofication of people in a non-gender specific way. When I bimbofy a population, I turn the women into vapid bimbos, the kind you read about in books and stories on the internet.

The men? While my movie theater example was one that included gender transformation, a town simply cannot operate with only bimbos as residents. There needs to be a male presence to run things, and to fuck those bimbos silly. So the men get an attitude adjustment and gain some considerable sexual stamina. Otherwise, I leave them alone. Operating this way, everyone will be very happy.

Just like I am addicted to bimbofication, I have helped make the local population addicted to coming to Blossom House. Those gifts I handed out to everyone who came to the grand opening? That was the catalyst. And the 40% of folks who didn't come. Well, they all got a special mailer. I'm sure I'll be seeing everyone else soon. And if someone is somehow immune? That's when I make a house call and fix the problem myself.

I could go into detail about the gift, but I do need to keep a low profile. Same for the mailer. I could say trade secrets, which is true to an extent, but the real answer is that if I come to your town to bimbofy it, I don't want you getting tipped off. Trust me, it's much more fun when you don't see it coming and your transformation appears natural, even if it is absolutely ridiculous if you stop to think about it. But you won't stop to think about it, because you will be too far gone by then.

Anyway, business was booming, even if we weren't actually making any money. A few tourists found their way in, but overall, I kept the place focused on the locals, catering to their needs and desires.

And even at this stage, I did nothing to the patrons. As long as they stopped in at least once a week, I was happy. For now, I wanted to make Blossom House a regular part of their lives.

So you might ask who I started to bimbofy then. My staff of course. It just so happened to be that I hired an all female staff. When I hired them, they just needed to be good at their jobs. I didn't need them to be good looking or anything else. Again, I was trying to show that I cared about the community and that I was catering to the locals.

The first step with my staff was to give them a gentle attitude shift. After two weeks of working for me, they could not stop smiling. While I didn't know for sure, I'm guessing many of them kept right on smiling in their sleep.

I like my bimbos to smile. I know some people prefer the permanent "O" shape for their mouths, but even the most brainless bimbo should look good and brainless with a smile plastered on her face.

The smiling is good for business too. Suddenly that early twenties woman who might have had a bit of an emo or goth look going, always looking like the world was going to end, is now smiling and spreading positivity. It's good for business and a good place to start in the bimbofication process.

Of course, my girls, as I tend to call them, get more than a smile in the first stage. I give their bodies a little boost too. Each one of them is different too. Ella had put on a few extra pounds and really struggled to shed them, no matter how hard she tried (in the big picture it wasn't very hard, but she tried nonetheless). Suddenly those pounds started to melt away. Of course she's happy about it.

Then there was Raven. She's the emo-goth girl. And her birth name really was Raven. It wasn't a self-chosen name. Although she did have naturally raven black hair. Raven got a boost in her bust, just a cup size or so. I also gave her hair some natural curl. No matter how much she tried to straighten it, it just wouldn't stay straight anymore. I was a little worried about the hair part, but the truth is, I think she liked it. I think she was living up to her name and the few changes I made allowed her to be more herself.

Brittney was the closest to a bimbo in town, which admittedly was not very close by my standards. She was already a blonde and pretty well stacked, but she had neither the attitude nor the style. And she had issues with anxiety that could at times be crippling. I freed her from her anxiety. She even told me how much she thought the job was helping her. How little she really understood.

I have three other girls who also work for me. Abigail, Nancy and Zella. Abigail is the bookworm of the bunch and she wears the thickest glasses I have ever seen. Or at least she did. She still wears them, but she took the glass out.

Nancy trained as a ballet dancer. She has a great limber body and her flexibility is unreal. Her only real problem was her acne. I could not say I'd ever seen a case so bad. Not anymore, however. Even her scars are starting to clear up.

Finally there is Zella. She was the one I needed to be careful with. Her dad was the local sheriff. I did not want to bring his wrath down on Blossom House if he noticed too big a change in his daughter. I should note right here that I don't do incest. Zella will never do anything sexual with the sheriff. My five other girls are welcome to let him fuck their brains out, but Zella will never take part.

With her father in mind, I decided to keep it simple at first, at least until I get him under my control too. Zella had always been short and to my surprise, she practically lived in flats. Usually the sub-five-foot club practically lived in heels, but not Zella. So that was the change I gave her. She has switched to heels. Over time I expect her to start wearing taller heels. I might also give her a little height boost further down the line, but I haven't decided yet.

I know that is not much yet, but damn does it feel good to finally get back to my bread and butter. I was getting tired of holding back while I got Blossom House set up. But now I can really start to have some fun.

ONE MONTH IN BLOSSOM

One month in and I still haven't touched my patrons at Blossom House.

Actually, that isn't entirely true. Sheriff Rawlins has made a few visits to Blossom House. In my last update I mentioned how he could pose a problem, since his daughter, Zella, works for me.

Not wanting to cause any issues with law enforcement, I decided my best bet was to make friends. Sheriff Rawlins is a friendly guy and an overall good person. I am sure he operates the Sheriff's Office with great integrity.

I certainly don't want to stop him from doing his job. I just don't want him to intervene when his daughter starts showing how much of a bimbo she can be. Dads are protective like that.

Suffice it to say, I don't think Sheriff Rawlins will be a problem for me or Zella. At least not anymore. He has loosened his leash on his daughter and now just wants her to be happy. And I can guarantee she will be happy. She will be too much of a bimbo not to be happy.

With Sheriff Rawlins out of the way, I should talk a little

more about my progress with the residents of Blossom. In only four weeks, I have turned 90% of the population into regular patrons. It helps that they eat and drink for free, but I have already made Blossom House the go-to place for the locals to hang out and enjoy themselves.

In celebration of this, I decided to close for a couple hours on a Monday, thus far our least busy day of the week, and throw ourselves a little party. With all the hard work my girls have been putting in, I thought they deserved it.

The music was blasting, the drinks were flowing and the girls were dancing. I played both DJ and bartender while the six girls enjoyed themselves, finally being able to cut loose at work and truly enjoy themselves.

Now, it's true that I might have helped them all along a little with getting into the partying mood. The combination of lowered inhibitions and increased arousal had all six girls brimming with energy. And with me being otherwise occupied with the music and the drinks, the girls turned to each other to satisfy their needs.

Of my little band of future bimbos, Ella has taken the mantle of leadership upon her shoulders. She was certainly the most outgoing to begin with, but also the least submissive. That is a trait she will find growing within her, but I like it when my girls form their own natural hierarchy. It's easier for me and it means I can have more fun with them all later when I find ways of introducing a little bit of bimbofying chaos.

With Ella acting as leader, it was only appropriate that she make the first move. She chose Raven as her first dance partner.

Both were dressed more provocatively than they usually did. Ella wore this tight little black dress that showed off how much weight she had lost. Raven was beginning to let go of her goth image. She wore a pink scoop neck top to show off her expanded cleavage and a white pencil skirt. The combination left a band of bare skin around her midsection.

Once those two began dancing, the other girls paired off too, but it was clear they were taking their cues from Ella.

It only took a couple more songs before Ella began making out with Raven. The two girls locked lips and began to explore each other's bodies with their hands. The music was merely background as their worlds had shrunk down to just the two of them in the moment.

Half an hour later, the six girls were in the middle of a full on sexual orgy. They were hot and horny and desperately needed relief. And relief they received. I cannot tell you how many times each girl came, but it is quite possible all six of them would need to also use their toes for counting that high, after using all 10 fingers. Not that any of them were keeping track.

Eventually the party wound down. All six girls were smiling with dopey, freshly climaxed grins. Clothing had been discarded in their fits of passion, leaving them all partially or, in Ella's case, fully nude.

Finally I felt comfortable calling my girls a family. They had bonded and would do anything for each other. It would be all the more important as they slowly descended into bimbodom. Bimbos need bimbo friends.

Once the party had ended, it only took about an hour to return Blossom House to a state where we could open. No one but us would know what the girls got up to. For the next week they would all add an extra smile whenever they acknowledged each other, both at work and out and about Blossom.

With my girls finding happiness in their jobs and each other, I finally felt like it is time to start bimbofying Blossom in earnest. I couldn't wait.

BIMBOFYING STARTS AT THE TOP

I finally started branching out and started bimbofying my patrons. My methodology is pretty simple. Whenever possible, start at the top.

With my girls, Ella has been pushed more than the others toward a bimbo ideal. She has already had to get bigger bras twice now to contain her expanding bust.

When it comes to my girls, I take care of them. I have connections and I make sure they are never left wanting when it comes to their changing bodies. Therefore, their need for new clothes to fit their changing bodies and their changing styles are supplied by me. They make the request of course, but they don't pay a cent for anything like that. They are my ambassadors of bimbodom.

As Ella was the leader of my girls, she led the way in terms of transformations. There was no longer any hint of the extra weight she carried around. As such, she started regularly wearing cropped tops to show off her taut midriff. She even got her belly-button pierced to further highlight what I think is her favorite feature. Although I expect her breasts will eventually take over as her favorite. She is coming along nicely in that department too.

The other girls are making progress too. But that is for another part of this story. Now we are talking about my first real steps in bimbofying Blossom.

Just like how Ella led the transformation of my girls, I looked to the head of the town to lead the changes in the residents. Therefore, I started with Mayor Danielle Harvest.

Mayor Harvest was both the youngest mayor Blossom had ever had and also the first woman to be elected mayor. I say that, because there had been instances where women took over the job on an interim basis, completing another mayor's term. I always do my research about the places I look to settle in.

Mayor Harvest was married to Jacob Harvest. They were a political duo in Blossom. While Mr. Harvest did not hold any office, he was viewed by the residents as a mover and a shaker in the community. That was a positive in my opinion.

Anytime you bimbofy a woman in power, it is important to plan for who will be in charge once she is no longer capable of wielding the power she has been given.

In this case, have Jacob ready to start making decisions worked perfectly. Not that Mayor Harvest was just going to walk away from the position. My goal was to keep her as the figurehead of Blossom. She would become Blossom's version of the Queen of England.

You might wonder how I went about bimbofying the mayor. She and her husband had both begun visiting Blossom House on a regular basis. They actually started joining us for dinner twice a week. They also both held lunch meetings at Blossom House, although separately.

In this particular situation, I started the process by inviting them to join me for a more private dinner, just the three of us. I had my girls serve us the best food I had available at the time. It was important to impress upon my guests for the evening that I valued them.

I also happened to make a few alterations to my guests. Anytime I bimbofy a town like this, I have to take it slow. I couldn't have Mayor Harvest walk out of Blossom House as a fully stereotypical bimbo with only sex on her mind. And it is the first steps that are always the most dangerous.

Knowing that it would be Jacob that would be taking over, even if Danielle technically remained the mayor, I decided to start priming them for just such an occurrence.

I increased Danielle's submissiveness, especially toward her husband. It would not be long before she would be turning to him to make the tough decisions she faced as mayor. It would start at home. She would turn to him whenever she had to sleep on a decision. Soon, however, I expected him to have his own office in Town Hall.

Likewise, I needed to turn up Jacob's dominance toward his wife, so that he would step up and make those decision she wanted him to. It would not work to just have her ask the questions if he was unwilling to provide the answers.

Of course, that was not all I did during our dinner. I gave Danielle a little physical boost, improving her skin, helping her lose a couple pounds and make her breasts a little more perky. Yes, soon she would look and act like a total bimbo, but not yet. But more importantly, I significantly increased Danielle's sex drive. Sex would become at least a daily event for her, and eventually more frequent than that.

Jacob also got a physical boost. Stronger muscles were the name of the game. I also gave him greater sexual stamina. He would have to keep up with his bimbo wife eventually.

When the husband and wife pair left Blossom House later that night, Jacob had his hand on his wife's ass. She certainly seemed to like his hand on her ass. They had been in several times before, but they had never used such public displays of affection.

Either way, I was happy with the results and I looked forward to bimbofying them further in the future.

EXPANDING BLOSSOM HOUSE

Two months in and I was ready to start expanding Blossom House. I had only started to bimbofy my patrons, but I am already finding the operation understaffed. Luckily I planned for this and have had several new girls getting ready to join Blossom House.

Blossom House is more than just a lounge where people can eat and drink, although that has been my primary focus in getting people to become regular patrons. As was true during the grand opening, we also offer various spa related services. Up until this point I had been contracting with local people and businesses, having them offer their services at Blossom House.

Since the beginning, contracting out these services was always going to be temporary. The contracts I signed all specified an end date. That end date had finally been reached and I now had several new girls ready to join my team.

One of my big selling points when I first arrived in Blossom and announced my intention of opening Blossom House was that I would invest in the local community.

Included in that was paying for the training and education of my work force.

The six girls who first started at Blossom do a combination of work in the restaurant and bar area and in the kitchen. They do not have the training to perform massages or spa facials or health and fitness coaching.

But I hired three other girls at the beginning that have not yet played a role in the Blossom House operation. You might ask where they have been, but the answer is quite simple. They were off-island getting their work education and training.

Of course, despite these other girls being off-site all this time, I still kept close tabs on them. Not only did I want to make sure that they were learning the skills and earning the certificates necessary to perform their future jobs, they were also on a much faster track to full bimbofication.

Jasmine was my new masseuse. She went away to become a licensed massage therapist. And I must already tell you, she is phenomenal at massage. When she first returned I asked her to show me what she had learned. Best massage I've ever had.

Originally, Jasmine was just an average girl in her early twenties. I do not know her ethnic background, since that is not something I particularly care about, but she had moderately dark skin and beautiful black hair. I am not someone who turns ethnicity into a fetish. When I first hired Jasmine, she appeared reasonably athletic, although not very fit. What I liked about her was the caring vibe I got from her. She truly wanted to help people. When I offered her the job, with the prerequisite training that I would pay for, she jumped at the chance.

The Jasmine who returned to Blossom looked a little different form the way she did when she left. Her athleticism had been enhanced, her body sleek and toned. Her breasts had more than doubled in size, however, and her ass has grown to almost match. When before, she was modest, now she is anything but. Her standard work uniform had become a skimpy bikini and a pair of shorts. Usually the button on the shorts was left undone, showing the top of her bikini bottoms, assuming she is wearing any that day. Her hair has also grown out straight down to her ass. She is a sight to see. And funnily enough, she has barely noticed the changes in herself. Then again, while Jasmine had become great at massage and was more than willing to provide a happy ending for her customers upon request, I would not trust her with much else, as she is pretty much a bimbo in every other respect now.

Violet joined the team as a life-long resident of Blossom. Her life was not going where she wanted it to, despite multiple attempts to right the ship. Her college plans were scuttled when her financial aid fell through. Then she tried her hand at becoming an artist. She had skilled hands, but after investing her life savings in painting supplies, she discovered she had developed an allergy to something in the paints she had purchased.

When I first met Violet, she was hitting the pavement, handing out her resume at every business in town. I had no idea why she got no leads. Maybe it was the purple hair. She did follow her namesake in choosing her hair color.

I saw right away that Violet had style. She had no money to truly be fashionable, but she did great work with what she had. And that was why I offered to send her to beauty school so she could work in my new salon. For the first time in her life, she found someone other than her family willing to invest in her. Of course she said yes.

Returning to Blossom after several months in school on the mainland, many would not recognize Violet. She still sported the purple hair, although it was now clearly a violet shade to match her name, but she otherwise looked like she had spent her whole life following fashion and modeling. All signs of having a rough go of adulting were gone. And what was more, she was fully versed in all aspects of running the Blossom House salon. Hair, makeup, nails, skincare, clothing and so much more were stored in her brain.

Of course, with her new skills, learned far faster than was normal, left her appearing rather dim about most other things. She was a beautiful girl, but she definitely was not going to be conversing with people about politics or complex social issues. She would be happy to talk your ear off about the latest trends in high heels, however.

Finally there was Madison. Her transformation was definitely the most extreme of anyone I had altered in Blossom thus far. Madison was a big girl, to put it mildly. I have no intention to body shame, but she was dangerously overweight, to the point her health was severely impacted.

I think everyone was surprised when I offered her the job to become the Blossom House fitness instructor, trainer and nutritionist, including her. She would have turned my offer down if I had not been so insistent. I can be very persuasive when I want to be.

Madison worked hard while she was gone, both in the classroom and in the gym. She of course believes that she made such a huge improvement in her health through diet and exercise alone, but that is the way I wanted it. She needed to believe just as much as her future clients would. Miracles really can happen.

The Madison who returned to Blossom was barely recognizable. All the extra weight was gone. She was what I would call a sporty bimbo, her preferred choice of outfit being a sports bra and either spandex shorts or tights. Her breasts very much looked fake, but I can assure you they were all natural. Her face also went through a significant change as she lost weight. Her lips remained plump, but her cheek bones became very prominent. Also, her once brunette hair was now nearly white and hung down her back in loose waves. That was when she wore her hair down. Usually it was up in a ponytail to accommodate her workout schedule.

I am sure people will question what happened to Madison while she was gone. The transformation was drastic. But other than the rumor of plastic surgery and other procedures to lose weight, they will be happy for her. She went from possibly the least healthy person in town to the most health conscious bimbo she could be. And her transformation will only attract others to join her in the Blossom House gym.

It felt good to bring the new girls into the fold. They were already overly aroused and happily bisexual, so they fit right in with the rest of my girls. I made sure to throw another little party for them on a slow Monday morning. They got their drink on and their sex on. It turned out Violet could be quite the screamer, especially when Jasmine was kneading her muscles and Ella was licking her pussy. The girls know how to have fun, I'll give them that.

Seeing them enjoy themselves definitely made me want to start turning up the arousal of my patrons. Sex was about to become a much more common aspect of life in Blossom.

THE MAYOR OF BLOSSOM GETS A MAKEOVER

It was a very relaxed and suggestible mayor that arrived at Blossom House and she continued to advance the changes that would eventually happen for her constituents.

One of the nice things about having an in-house salon and spa at Blossom House is how easy it is to make changes that people don't fully notice. It's easier to explain away a change after a visit.

This is the story of Mayor Harvest's first visit to the Blossom House salon and the results of her makeover.

Danielle, as she preferred me to call her, began her visit with a massage. Jasmine worked her magic on the mayor, kneading her muscles and releasing all the tension that she had built up trying to make those hard decisions that mayors are expected to make.

The mayor laid down on the table, face down with a towel over ass. She still wore panties. That would eventually change, but I was in no hurry. At some point she would probably start to forget to put them on in the first place.

Jasmine wore her usual work uniform, something she chose for herself. On that day she had chosen a red triangle bikini that barely contained her large tits. She wore matching bikini bottoms, but one would only know that because of the open button on her little jean shorts and the tie sides of the bottoms popping over the top of the shorts. She looked absolutely scrumptious, but when it came to her clients, she was entirely professional. Or at least she was then. She had no qualms about finishing her massages with a happy ending for her clients, but that would not begin for a few weeks still. Her clients, male and female, needed to be properly prepared before she could take that step.

It was a very relaxed and suggestible Danielle who made her way from Jasmine's massage studio to Violet's salon. Violet was looking on-point as she now always did, her outfit figure hugging and contrasting nicely with her name-sake colored hair.

Danielle only wore a robe over her panties at this point and she was relaxed enough to let her robe hang more open that she normally would have. Not that she was revealing anything, but Danielle had always appeared modest and conservative in the way she dressed.

As soon as Violet got Danielle in her chair, she went straight to work. Danielle was asked to approve all of the changes to her appearance, or at least most of them, but in her state, she readily agreed with her stylist.

Blonde hair? Of course, that sounded splendid. What Danielle did not know was the color change was permanent. She would forever more, or at least until Violet or myself changed it, be a blonde. What was more, the change would leave her hair gradually getting lighter until she was a perfect platinum blonde. But that would take several months. Although it would be helped along by well above average hair growth rate.

With the color change came a change in style too. Danielle kept her hair in a short bob. It was professional and easy enough to maintain. That wouldn't do for the bimbo mayor. When Danielle finally left, her hair would be noticeably longer. With Violet's help, she would continue to grow it out until it was quite long. The amount of work it would take to maintain would be large, but once her husband began taking on many of the mayoral duties, it would all be fine.

Obviously, the hair does not make the bimbo. Danielle's makeover would require far more than just a change to her hair. Next up on Violet's checklist was Danielle's nails. The mayor kept her finger nails short, maintaining a professional appearance and making it easy to work with her hands, typing and writing mainly.

Of course, in her suggestible state, Violet easily persuaded Danielle that long nails would be better. They certainly looked better and looking good helped one feel good, even in situations when she felt like she was in over her head. Especially in those situations. Danielle nodded in agreement as if Violet spoke some previously undiscovered truth. The world made so much more sense that way.

After the nails came makeup. Danielle had only used makeup sparingly throughout her life, even on her wedding day. That was about to change. Danielle was about to find out that she hated the idea of ever being seen without an immaculately made up face. Violet walked her client through every step, making sure Danielle understood each and every part of her new routine.

As part of the makeup process, Violet used a special product I had developed that caused eye lashes to grow long and thick. Danielle would never need false lashes, but many would think she used them.

Danielle stared at her reflection, wide-eyed. She had never seen herself look this way, but with Violet's encouraging words, she knew that this was the real her. Yes, it would take an hour or more to get ready to leave the house, but that was a small price to pay for looking as she did now.

Still, however, the makeover was not yet complete. Violet was not only fully versed as a hair stylist, but she had trained in various spa techniques too.

While Danielle was still in her suggestible state, it was easy to talk the future bimbo into a full body makeover. Soon the mayor was standing fully nude in the middle of the room with her arms held out slightly from her body, her robe and panties sitting on the salon chair.

Violet began by using a special process of mine that permanently removed body hair. It is a process that resembles both waxing and laser hair removal. Violet began by spreading a sweet smelling paste all over Danielle's body. Every inch of her body was coated, from her neck to her toes, leaving her now long finger nails alone.

Then came a special laser-like device that appeared to melt the paste into the skin. This isn't fully accurate, but it is close enough for my descriptions here. Trade secrets and all. The final step is to remove the "melted" paste, pulling it away from the skin, much like waxing.

The result is a hair free body, but also healthier skin. This process can also remove unwanted tattoos and even birthmarks. In fact, Danielle had a birthmark on her left ass cheek. After the treatment, her skin was completely flawless as well as hairless.

I used this time to also make a few other changes to Danielle through my own means. I figured any changes she notices could be explained away with the makeover. Not that she would be complaining.

First and foremost, I gave Danielle a true boost to her breasts. She came into Blossom House wearing a single letter bra. She would need double letters from now on. And what was more, she would be happy about it too.

I also reshaped Danielle's ass, giving it tone and size. It would be something men would stare at as she walked away from them, it swaying back and forth with each step.

I also gave her another round of toning up all around, smoothing out her overall figure to a more hour glass shape. What can I say? I wanted a classic bimbo as the leader of my bimbofied town.

After Danielle's body was reshaped, there was still the matter of her clothing style. To begin with, the clothes she came in with would never fit her properly. Her bra and panties were too small for her transformed figure. Her blouse and pants would still fit, but the proportions would be off. They would be tight across her breasts and ass, but loose everywhere else. She needed something different to wear.

Again, Violet led the charge, suggesting a whole new style for the mayor. Her simple cotton bra was be replaced by something lacy and lifting, making her cleavage even more prominent. Her similarly cotton panties were replaced by a lacy thong, matching her bra. Violet impressed upon the mayor the importance of matching underwear, assuming underwear was worn. Both girls giggled at Violet's statement, although I knew at that moment, Violet was wearing neither.

When it came time to find a more appropriate outfit, Violet once again had all the answers for the relaxed, suggestible, and slightly confused mayor. Her white blouse was replaced by a pink fitted blouse that was perfectly designed for her new figure. Not that the new blouse was capable of closing around her expanded bust. But that meant she showed plenty of cleavage. Violet really hammered home the importance of showing off cleavage, describing it as showing her worth in every situation. Danielle ate it up.

Instead of black pants, Violet put the mayor in a tight black skirt. Its length was mostly professional, reaching down almost to her knees, but the long slit showed far more leg than Danielle had ever been known to show. Again, Violet impressed upon her client the importance of showing off such nice legs. It was especially important in the high heels she needed to wear.

The shoes again pushed Danielle in a new direction. She has always kept her wardrobe simple, including her shoes, often choosing flats. When heels were necessary, she kept them low. That was all a thing of the past. Tall heels were in, Violet had explained. The taller the better. The mayor took this new knowledge in, internalizing it until it was the absolute truth. She would never wear flats or low heels again, she promised herself.

It was spring and still cool at times. Instead of a full length jacket, Danielle was given a small bolero jacket, too small to close and too short to do anything more than frame her chest and keep her arms warm. Still, Danielle loved it.

The final step was to change up the mayor's jewelry. Her wedding band and engagement ring were already impressive, demonstrating the wealth of her husband. To complete Danielle's new look, Violet provided the mayor with large hoop earrings and a new necklace of a flower blossom that sat perfectly nestled in her cleavage.

When Mayor Harvest left Blossom House that day, she looked like a bimbo trying to look professional, but always seeming to fail in everything she did. Despite that, Danielle was proud of her new look and kept expressing her thanks to Jasmine, Violet, and myself for all that we did for her.

As she left, the relaxed state she had been in throughout the makeover was beginning to wear off. However, she was still out of it just enough to admit that she would be heading home for a quickie before she returned to the office. She was too horny to make it through the rest of her day.

Everyone was smiling, myself included, as Mayor Danielle Harvest left Blossom House that day, tottering in her heels, her cheeks flushed with arousal, as she made her way home to fuck her husband.

As much as I wanted to drink to my success, I still had work to do. For the new Danielle to hold beyond the day, she needed reinforcement. Namely, she needed a new wardrobe and beauty supplies. By the end of the day, she would receive a large delivery of both. But those items still needed packing.

A bimbofier's job is never over.

8

THE FIRST BIMBOFICATION
PROBLEM IN BLOSSOM

Something went wrong. Specifically, something went wrong with Mayor Harvest, or Danielle as she is better known in Blossom House.

Everything seemed to go well after Danielle's spa day. She left looking like a blonde bimbo attempting to look and act professional, but struggling to keep it together.

And everything seemed to continue in that manner for several days. I made it a point to check in with Danielle regularly, always having some reason or another to contact her, visit her office, or even swing by her home. She seemed to be embracing her new look and attitude.

But that suddenly changed on Day 5. I stopped by Danielle's office to pick up some paperwork relating to the eventual expansion of Blossom House. Instead of the blonde almost bimbo mayor I found Danielle to look exactly like her former self. The pantsuit had returned, as had the brunette hair. Even her tits were back to their former size.

Quite frankly, I was shocked. I had not seen a reversion like this in many years. And definitely not when using my latest techniques. It would be one thing for her to shake off a part of the changes Violet and I made to her, but it looked like she had completely reverted to her previous non-bimbofied state.

Not wanting to appear too interested in the sudden changes in the mayor, I casually asked Danielle's secretary about he mayor's recent shifts in style.

"I don't get it," the secretary said. "She showed up with blonde hair and acting like an airhead for a couple days. Then she was completely back to normal when she came in this morning. I know she's on some medications, but that couldn't explain the sudden hair color changes and the fluctuations in her breasts."

I had never seen my bimbofication processes and products ever interacting with medications before, but stranger things had happened before. I knew right then that I would need to do more research about our mayor before I made my next attempt.

"I bet dealing with your boss can be hard sometimes," I told the secretary. "You should come by Blossom House for a spa day. It's free for Blossom residents."

"Wow, that's really great," the secretary said. "I might just have to do that. I've only stopped in for a drink occasionally, but I've always really liked it there. Do I need to make an appointment?"

"How does Friday night sound? I'd say Saturday, but you'll want to enjoy as much of your weekend as you can after a nice relaxing spa experience, especially after a week like this one, right..."

I paused, realizing I never got the secretary's name. It was important to learn my patrons' names.

"Katherine," the secretary said, blushing a little. "And thank you. I'll come by right after work on Friday. If I'm lucky, the mayor will let me leave early."

"I look forward to seeing you."

You might wonder why I so quickly turned my attention to Katherine, rather than dig deeper with Danielle right then. The simple fact was, I did not yet know exactly where to begin with the mayor. Something had caused a complete or near-complete reversion. Such an event was rare and I did not want to walk to get myself over my head.

It is the early stages of a bimbofication of a town like Blossom that can be the most dangerous in my experience. I did not want to tip my hand too much. It was possible Danielle already suspected me for her "odd" week. I did not want my investigations to bring further attention upon me and Blossom House.

However, I saw no reason why I could not begin to stack the cards against the mayor by bimbofying her staff. The more I made bimbohood seem normal to the mayor, the less likely she would revert in the future. At least that was my working theory. Changing normality can be the biggest step in getting people to accept a new way of life. Creating a new normal, as you will.

And so I began work to figure out what happened to Danielle. Maybe her husband would give me a clue?

9

BLOSSOM MAYORAL UPDATE

It had been two days and I was no closer working out what caused Danielle's reversion. Actually, that is not entirely true. I had ruled out a reaction to any medication she was taking.

I could go into how I learned about the contents of the mayor's medicine cabinet, but you really do not want to know the details. It's funny how I am perfectly happy to describe how I have gone about bimbofying people. In that regard, I live in a gray area. But some of my tactics would not pass muster in a police investigation and are quite likely illegal in the vast majority of civilized places in this world.

Having eliminated Danielle's medications as the cause of her reversion, I still had just about every other possibility to explore. For all I knew she had a genetic anomaly that significantly lowered her susceptibility to the bimbofication process. Obtaining a DNA sample would not be difficult, but the process of having it analyzed was not easy. There was not a 23andMe available to bimbofiers like myself.

Despite the overall lack of progress with the mayor,

Katherine was a completely different story. She is starting to come along very nicely.

Katherine arrived at Blossom House straight from work on that first Friday. She got off work an hour early, just so she could spend more time in the spa and salon.

I had been subtle with some aspects of Danielle's bimbofication. I was not about to do the same with Katherine.

From the moment Katherine walked into Blossom House that afternoon, she was on her way to being the best bimbo secretary Blossom had ever known.

In this case, it all started with her mind. Katherine turned out to have been a reasonably smart young woman. Had she grown up in a city and not on a rural island, she likely would have gone to graduate school, maybe even trained to be a lawyer or a doctor. But the simple fact is, a bimbo secretary only needs a brain when it comes to doing her work. Every other aspect of her life should be care free and full of glitter and sparkles.

So from the moment Katherine walked into Blossom House, I went to work on her mind. I did not even bother making her suggestible during her massage with Jasmine. However, much like the massage she did receive, I spent her visit massaging her mind, molding it and transforming it to meet new specifications.

Katherine essentially was left with two states of mind. There was Katie, the bimbo secretary. She might be slow, especially when it came to typing, but she was loyal and always eager to please her boss, the mayor. When it came to her job, she would be the best secretary she could.

Outside of work, that was the realm of Kitty, the sexy bimbo who's only thoughts revolved around looking pretty and satisfying her epic libido. And I should emphasize that at work, she will prefer to use the name Katie, but outside of work, she will prefer the name Kitty. It is possible the two parts of her could be fused down the line, but I do want her to be capable at her day job.

So with Katherine's mind worked out, that left her body. And what can I say, I do enjoy the classic bimbo look of big tits, a big ass and a tiny little waist. Actually, to be completely honest, I prefer a well toned ass to a big ass. But in this case, I chose to go with the classic.

As the workweek was over, it was Kitty who walked out of Blossom House that day. She looked absolutely stunning in the little maroon dress we gave her. The dress barely went past the swell of her ass and the neckline showed off about as much cleavage as it could while still remaining acceptable for the future streets of Blossom.

Kitty was very thankful of the services we provided her. She seemed so much happier than when I had seen her in the office. We at Blossom House had literally taken away her worries and fears and replaced them with a sexy submissive confidence and an oversized libido. She was desperate to thank me and my girls.

One would think that I would do all this out of a selfish desire to be pleasured, but I really don't. And as an example of this, I abstained from Kitty's offer, but I made sure each of my girls got a bonus from the latest bimbo of Blossom. I could hear the orgasmic screams in my office. As a note, I may need to add additional sound proofing to the interior walls. I don't want visiting tourists to get the wrong impression of Blossom House. Yes, sexual services will be offered to some people, but I have not nor will I ever operate a brothel.

Returning to the new bimbo, now that Kitty is free to be her bimbo self, I will need to start working on the rest of the staff in the mayor's office. Even if I discover the cause of Danielle's reversion, I do not plan to make another attempt until she is the cherry on top of the bimbo sundae that is her office. But until that time, Kitty/Katie will need some new bimbo friends both in and out of the office.

10

BRINGING MY GIRLS INTO THE FOLD

At a certain point, the number of people in on the plan needs to increase. After having been in operation for a few months I had decided it was finally time to tell my staff the master plan.

By this point, they were all well on their way to being bimbos, if they weren't there already. The latest additions, namely Jasmine, Madison and Violet, were basically as bimbofied as they're going to get. But my original girls had all slowly worked their way down the path toward full bimbos.

Ella continued to be the leader, including of the new girls. She had this dominant streak, at least as far as with the other girls, that meant all I needed to do is give her a direction and she made sure all the other girls were on board.

In addition to being the leader of my girls, she also led the way in popularizing the latest changes I made to my bimbo staff. What that means is Ella now had by far the biggest tits of the bunch. I also knew she had about three guys in regular rotation. She often got picked up at the end of her shifts by one of the three. She was pretty open with the other girls about all the fucking around she did.

Promiscuous bimbos are not specifically my thing, but it can be one side effect of turning up a girl's libido. I generally figure as long as a girl does not cast a bad light on my operation, I don't care what she does during her free time. If Ella wants to spend each night fucking a different guy, who am I to complain? As long as she is happy and safe, I'm all for it.

Raven had unofficially become Ella's second in command. She primarily works behind the bar. First off, she no longer resembles a goth in any way. Sure, her hair is still black and her name is Raven, but that is it. She has a mass of black curls that, if straight, would reach her now bubbled ass, but since her hair will not stay straight, it falls to her mid-back.

With the goth image gone, Raven has elected to go in the exact opposite direction. She wears nothing but bright colors in hyper-feminine styles. She makes it a point to show off the curves she has developed, with tight fitting clothes that show off plenty of leg and as much cleavage as she can get away with. I can't remember the last time I remember seeing her wear a bra.

Since Raven spends the vast majority of her time behind the bar, she has developed a flirty attitude. She mixes great drinks, but more importantly, she leaves the patrons with a big smile on their faces. And with her being fully bisexual, she finds away to flirt with everyone who comes in. She's already up to four marriage proposals while working behind the bar. Somehow she's even good at turning people down.

Brittney is the dumbest of the bunch. It's a good thing we don't charge money, because I'm pretty sure she can't do math at this point. But Brittney makes up for her lack of intelligence with energy and giggles. You'd be amazed at how well she gets along with people, even the smartest people in Blossom, with those two characteristics. At least it is obvious she doesn't have a thought in her head. Her eyes have a vapid blankness to them that I have never seen before, even in my many, many years of experience.

Nancy remains the most flexible of my girls, although she has no interest in the ballet anymore. Most days she primarily works in the kitchen, but she has been known to come out and entertain the guests with her hyper-sexual dance moves. One nice thing about having the whole town adjusting to bimbo characteristics being the norm, they don't mind and even enjoy the increased sexuality that everyday life brings. If I were operating a strip club, Nancy would be the first girl to volunteer. I think she would work for free, just for the opportunity to dance in front of people. Despite having the assets of a stripper, I prefer to keep things classy at Blossom House.

Abigail continues to wear her glasses, although, as I mentioned before, she has taken the actual glass out of them. As the original bookworm of the bunch, Abigail has taken that aspect of her personality to the extreme. Now she puts her emphasis on being a sexy schoolgirl, with the short tartan skirts, knee high socks, a blouse she ties off under her tits and a little tie that sits perfectly in her cleavage. I tried calling her Abby once, but she practically scolded me, telling me that no one would ever take her seriously as a student unless she used her full name of Abigail. We both laughed, acknowledging the game she played. Abigail also primarily works in the kitchen.

Finally there is Zella. As the Sheriff's daughter, I had been nervous initially about hiring her. It was the Sheriff who I first altered, making him happy for his daughter, no matter what life choices she chose for herself. As it turned out, she has discovered a bad girl streak in her. Personally, I think it was introducing her to the heels. Leather has become her favorite clothing material. She regularly wears high heeled leather boots and the tightest leather pants I can find for her. She also wears this cropped leather jacket. It has no hope of ever closing around her tits, but it goes with her overall look. Of course, Zella has also developed an oral fixation. Maybe its to help make up for her height, but she constantly has something in her mouth. Most of the time it is gum, but she is happy to replace that with a cock. I hear she is also the best at eating the pussies of my girls too.

With the changes to the girls nearly complete (I might still make a few tweaks here or there), it was finally time to let them in on the secret. Despite them being bimbos, I knew I could trust them to keep a secret. The simple fact was, I had the ability to limit what they talked about with others, so I was not concerned about the secret getting out.

I held a staff meeting, sitting all nine of my girls down to have a little talk with them. I could have continued keeping them in the dark, but I knew our work would be much more effective if I had access to their eyes and ears. I could not be everywhere, nor could I track everything on the many cameras I had installed in Blossom House.

I started by asking how much they enjoyed being my bimbos. At various points I had used the word to describe each of them in private conversations, although I had never used it with them as a group. They all nodded their heads and smiled. Brittney giggled. I couldn't be sure she really understood, but that was okay. I was pretty sure she wouldn't remember half of this anyway.

Then I went into my story, how I set up Blossom House to bimbofy the town. All the girls watched me with rapt attention, taking in my every word as if it were gospel. I explained how they were the first girls in town to be given my gift. That certainly made them feel special.

From there it was easy for me to ask for their help. I gave them the whole eyes and ears speech. If they saw someone behaving strangely or overheard people talking about the changes in town, they were to come to me immediately. I needed to know if we were going to turn all the girls in town into bimbos.

The girls definitely liked hearing that. I could see the wheels of their minds turning, even Brittney's, as they processed the information. They all came to the conclusion that being a bimbo was the best thing ever and that all the girls in town should be bimbos too. I do love bimbo logic.

With that part of the meeting concluded, I decided it was only fair to give the girls a little playtime. Making a bimbo sit still like that is like punishment for them. It was time to reward them for their attentiveness.

BLOSSOM MAYORAL UPDATE 2

A quick update about the mayor of Blossom. I have unfortunately still not figured out why Danielle Harvest reverted to her pre-bimbo form, but I had a feeling I was close. Possibly less than a week before I had it worked out.

There were two developments, however.

First, Kitty/Katie has been sending the mayor into fits. She can still do her job, but the rumors are that Katie has been letting a bit more of Kitty slip into her time in the office than I had originally planned.

I am actually not at all concerned about this. I've read the bylaws of Blossom and firing a town employee is very difficult. The likelihood of Kitty/Katie losing her job is slim.

Moreover, my eventual plan was to have Kitty take over full time. Her grabbing the spotlight a little early doesn't bother me in the slightest.

Second, the fur has been flying in the Harvest household, or so the rumor mill tells me. It seems that while my initial changes to Danielle did not last when she reverted, they did last in her husband, Jacob.

Apparently, he has been upset about the balanced nature of their relationship. He loved it when Danielle was in bimbo mode, but now that she's back to normal, he is unhappy.

Of course, likewise, Danielle is unhappy because Jacob has been trying to tilt the balance of their relationship in his favor. Jacob was only doing what he thought is right. Obviously, I was the one who shifted Jacob's perspective.

Again, I am not particularly worried. Even if they do split for some reason, neither of them are leaving Blossom anytime soon. And once I bimbofy Danielle again, I can easily get them to reconcile. Small town gossip certainly is fun.

Hearing all this great gossip did give me an idea that I had not previously thought of before. Blossom has a small newspaper. The Blossom Courier was a weekly publication staffed by mostly women. It made for a great bimbofication target as it could be used as a means to push the bimbo agenda around town.

When bimbofying a whole town, there are certain rules I tend to follow, but the game plan can vary a lot. And most importantly, one cannot be afraid to call an audible occasionally. The mayor needs bimbofying soon, but the Blossom Courier just moved up the list on where to strike next.

MAKING A BLOSSOM HOUSE CALL

Zella came to me with a problem. She was so cute, trying to act like a badass in her leather pants and jacket, but at the same time being the submissive bimbo she really is and how much she craves attention.

"Like, my friend Shaniqua came home from college and she doesn't like me anymore," she had explained.

I sat Zella down and had her explain everything to me. It was a good thing I have learned patience, because trying to get information out of bimbos can be tough sometimes. Zella was no exception. She babbled away taking me on quite a journey as her story meandered about. She nearly distracted herself from her own story five separate times. I can't complain though. I did make her this way, after all.

The short version of the story is this. Shaniqua was a friend of Zella's who had left the island for school. During the summers she would work at the ice cream shop next to the ferry landing. It is a popular place with tourists. The reason Shaniqua has come up is that she has returned to Blossom. Apparently she has finished school and is exploring her options.

And it should be no surprise that the new Zella does not really match with her studious friend these days. Zella spends her time showing off and sucking cock instead of pretty much everything else. Suffice it to say, she and Shaniqua don't have much in common anymore.

The biggest risk in bimbofying a whole town is dealing with the peripheral people. That is, the people who have a connection to the town, but are not regular residents. Since they only get occasional snapshots, they are likely to be the ones who cause the most problems.

Shaniqua was the first person to pose any problems for me in that regard, so the fact we were already several months in, I figured we were doing pretty well. But she would require my immediate attention.

Ever since I told all my girls about my plans, they have been very supportive of the townsfolk. Without saying anything damaging to me or Blossom House, they have been great about pushing our patrons to behave in a more bimbo fashion.

In this specific case, Zella ended her long story with a simple enough request. "I just wish Shaniqua could be a bimbo like me." How could I turn her down?

The simplest way to deal with the problem that Shaniqua posed was to make a house call. I was sure the two of us could come to an agreement. In most situations I try and sit back and control things from a distance, wanting to limit my personal exposure. However, in this case, I believed it prudent to intervene personally to make sure we had a positive result.

Anytime I make a house call, I need to go into the situation with as much information as possible. I do my research, because I don't like surprises.

Shaniqua, as you might be able to guess, was black. Her family was one of the few black families in Blossom. I do have to admit, Blossom seriously lacks diversity. It is very white. And while I realize the stereotypical bimbo tends to be a white girl with big tits, blonde hair and either a stupid or surprised look on her face, I embrace diversity and love playing up a girl's natural features for a unique end result.

Shaniqua's family had already become regular patrons at Blossom House. While her parents and older brother showed no outward changes, they had already reached the point where they accepted the changes I was making to the people in town without question. And that would help a lot once I bimbofied Shaniqua.

Zella had already tried to get Shaniqua to visit Blossom House. But that only seemed to make Shaniqua dig in her heels. She refused, even after her family urged her to drop in and check the place out.

Since Shaniqua was living at home, I made an offer to her family. They would get a special dinner at Blossom House and I would take the big stick out of Shaniqua's ass. They jumped at the opportunity. In almost every family relationship there comes a time when adult children begin to clash with their parents, especially when they are all living under one roof.

As soon as Shaniqua's family arrived at Blossom House, I went to see Shaniqua. I knocked on the door. Shaniqua answered and I talked my way in the door. I was honest in so far as telling her that I was there on behalf of Zella, emphasizing that Zella hated what had come between them.

Shaniqua stood there wearing a simple tank top and a pair of pajama pants. She was clearly planning a night in and had figured it unlikely she would have visitors.

It was not long before we were both sitting in the living room and Shaniqua was pouring her heart out to me about how much Zella had changed and how it had ruined their friendship.

"She's so different now," Shaniqua said. "I mean, she looks really different. She looks like she went and got implants and lip fillers, because her boobs are huge on her tiny frame and her lips are really big too. And then there's the way she dresses now. All she seems to wear are high heels, the tightest leather pants I've ever seen and leather jackets over a cropped and low cut top.

"And then there's her behavior. I swear she doesn't have an original thought left in her head. And she acts really slutty too. Whenever she's not talking about how great Blossom House is, she is talking about looking hot and sucking dick. I don't understand how she changed so much in so short a time."

Shaniqua was nearly in tears when she added, "I just wish we could be friends like we used to be."

I had a hard time disguising my smile. I loved how Shaniqua had phrased her wish. If I were not already well past the point where the ethics of bimbofication bothered me, I would have at least been able to find a way to satisfy my conscience and find a way to make them friends again.

"What if Zella likes the way she is now?" I asked, skirting the line between playing devil's advocate and acting as a therapist.

"How can she?" Shaniqua snapped. "She's just a dumb slut now. I can't believe her dad lets her do what she does."

"Maybe he's just happy that she is happy," I said. "Is it wrong to do the things that make you happy as long as they don't cause others trouble or pain?"

"Well, no," Shaniqua answered almost immediately. She was a well trained feminist. Yes, she recognized women could be whoever they wanted and do whatever they wanted, but she still felt that women who acted like sluts were betraying women everywhere.

"So then what's the problem between you two?" I asked.

For whatever reason, I wanted her to say it, even though it would not be long before whatever friction she felt with Zella was a thing of the past. The simple fact was, by the time I left that house, Shaniqua was going to be just as big a bimbo as Zella.

"I guess we just grew apart," Shaniqua said. She sat there with her shoulders hunched looking dejected. Her defiance that had fed her up until now was gone. In its place was just sadness.

"Have no fear, because I can solve your problem," I said. "You and Zella can be the best of friends again, I promise."

Shaniqua did not say anything, but she looked up at me with hope in her eyes. I could tell that she would do anything to have her friends back.

"It's really simple, Shaniqua," I explained as I began my work. "We just need to expand your horizons a little. Let's start with your tits."

To say that Shaniqua was startled with how the conversation changed would be an understatement. However, before she had a chance to complain, her attention was drawn to her chest. Her breasts began to balloon up under her top, stretching it out to the point it looked ready to burst.

"That's a good start, don't you think?" I asked, not expecting an answer. Shaniqua's mouth made movements like she was about to say something, but she could not find the words. I couldn't blame her. I would have trouble speaking, let alone thinking, if I were in her position.

"But now that I see you have a nice rack, let's balance you out. I'm not into the big ass that black women get stereotyped with, but I think we can still pack something into that rear of yours. I bet you'll like getting your rear stuffed when we're all done here."

And with that, Shaniqua's ass started to grow. I kept it

muscular and firm. It was the kind of ass one earned in the gym from thousands of squats over a long period of time.

"What are you doing to me?" Shaniqua whined, finally finding her voice.

"I'm just giving you what you need so you and Zella can be friends again. When we're done here, you two can be bbff's. Best bimbo friends forever."

From there I continued shaping Shaniqua's body, sculpting her midsection, her legs, her arms. I even changed her feet so she would forever more either walk in heels or walk on her tiptoes. She and Zella might not be able to share shoes, but they should share an affinity for high heels. They were to be best friends again, after all.

Choosing what to do with Shaniqua's face and hair were more difficult. I definitely plumped up her lips, but not to the degree I did with Zella. She gets to be the Blossom blowjob queen. That's not to say that Shaniqua won't be sharing with her friend on occasion.

Black hair has always been tricky for me. I know what a pain it is to do certain styles with it. However, I can provide certain solutions. In the end I opted for long straight hair. While I knew such hair could be difficult to care for I figured it would look best with her new sense of style. And I can arrange it to make it easier to care for.

Of course, altering Shaniqua's body only takes her so far. By the time I was done making physical alterations, I could tell Shaniqua was close to tears again. She had given up any ideas of stopping me. But I could tell she had not yet embraced this new her.

"Do you want to look in the mirror before the next step?" I asked.

Shaniqua had the sniffles as her eyes watered. Sometimes the women I bimbofy like this just want to get it over with.

Others secretly want to see their new bodies before I take away their minds.

Shaniqua nodded her head.

I pulled her to her feet by her shoulders and guided her toward the bedrooms. She directed me toward her room where there was a full length mirror on the closet door.

The moment Shaniqua saw her reflection, I knew I had her. As much as she wanted to be sad about her predicament, I could tell she was secretly happy with the changes I had made to her body. She stood up tall, thrusting out her chest. Her tank top no longer met her pants, leaving a belt of taught skin visible. That was all to do with her tits, which strained against the fabric. Her hard nipples were clearly visible.

Shaniqua turned her body to get a look at her new ass. It was nice and round without dominating her features. Her loose fitting pajama pants pulled tight across is, making one think of yoga pants.

Of course, Shaniqua did not notice how she stood there on her toes. I'm not sure she had even realized I had altered the structure of her legs and feet so that her heels would not touch the ground. It was not a matter of pain. She simply could not stand flat footed.

"You look great this way," I said, trying to keep her spirits up. "But to be best friends with Zella again, we need to make some other changes."

She looked at me trying to figure out what I meant. She had no idea that I had already started making wholesale changes to her mind.

There are many ways to bimbofy a person's mind. With Shaniqua, I decided to start with a trim. First I cut away some of her processing power. If she could, she would realize she was a little slower. It took her longer to connect ideas, to comprehend words and whatnot.

Then I trimmed certain memories, namely the facts she

had learned in college. She was not going to need to have dates and places memorized as a bimbo. After that, I started trimming her inhibitions. I did not want her to be reckless, but removing her hangups, especially when it came to sex and sexuality was important.

At this point, Shaniqua could be described as a little slow on the uptake with a poor memory of academic facts who did not let societal judgments affect her decision making.

But there was still more to do. For everything I cut away, I needed to add something back, although not necessarily in equal amounts. I replaced Shaniqua's processing power with a desire to have fun. I replaced her academic memories with information related to fashion and sex. And then I replaced her inhibitions with a libido that could drive a nun to breaking her vows.

With most of the big changes complete, I focused on smaller changes. Yes, I did give her an affinity for anal sex. She had a nice ass and now she liked it when guys fucked it hard. Or when a girl wore a strap-on. She wasn't too picky in that regard.

"Thanks so much for making me a bimbo," Shaniqua said once we were done. She still wore her same outfit, but she definitely no longer looked like her old self. She was a hot little bimbo who was going to enjoy her new life.

However, I didn't feel like I could just leave Shaniqua there. For one, she needed new clothes. She would probably drive herself crazy trying to find clothing to fit her new style. So I brought her to Blossom House. She seemed completely willing to go now.

Not wanting to show her off too soon, I snuck her in the back and I took her to find some new clothes. I let her pick out two outfits. One was for tonight when we introduced the bimbo her to her family and to Zella. But I figured she needed something to wear at work. I fully intended to encourage her to continue working at the ice cream shop. That was about the best job she would be able to hold down.

For the ice cream shop, Shaniqua chose a simple dress with a belt to accentuate her waist that left plenty of cleavage and leg bare without being too slutty. She would be serving tourists, so she couldn't go overboard. She of course chose a pair of high heels.

For her debut outfit, Shaniqua focused on the risqué. She chose a tiny little skirt that hugged her ass and not much else. It would be clear if she bent over that she was not wearing panties. Her top was even bolder. She found a flimsy piece of fabric with two sleeves and stings to tie it. When she wore it, the top basically draped over her tits. A gust of wind or really any kind of movement risked exposing her tits to everyone. She definitely had the hot bimbo slut act down pat.

When I walked Shaniqua in to meet her family, and Zella who happened to be serving them at the moment, almost no one recognized her. She shuffled across the room and first gave Zella a big hug, telling her how excited she was to be able to be her friend again. Then she thanked her family for putting up with her before. Everyone wore a smile on their face.

That is how Shaniqua became a bimbo. She and Zella are great friends again and everything should work out perfectly for the new bimbo. Although I may need to pay a call to the ice cream shop to smooth things over. I would not be surprised if Shaniqua found herself enjoying standing over the open freezers to make her nipples hard. It would be like the new her to do something like that, I think.

INTRODUCING THE MAYOR OF BLOSSOM

"I would now like to introduce the bimbo mayor of Blossom, Dani Harvest," I said over the PA at the private party hosted at Blossom House. Music started to play and out walked the mayor in all her bimbodom to massive cheers and applause.

I suppose I'm getting ahead of myself. If you can't guess already, I finally solved the mystery behind the mayor's reversion to her non-bimbo state. The whole situation is rather technical, but it all came down to a worry stone the mayor carried almost everywhere with her. I'm guessing that if I started talking about radiation and DNA and whatnot, your eyes would start to glaze over, so I'm just not going to go there.

Once I identified the stone as the problem, it was easy enough to arrange for the mayor to lose it. Kitty was a big help with that.

With the setback that Danielle Harvest's reversion caused, I decided to make up for lost time with a big event. I had originally created some slow acting changes in the mayor conversion. Her hair was going to gradually lighten until she was a platinum blonde. The process would have taken months. But after her reversion, I decided to go all in and make all her changes at once.

My decision to make wholesale changes all at once was buoyed by the positive responses to the other bimbofications in town. My girls have become big hits around town. They weren't celebrities by any means, but everyone seems to like them.

That is also true of Shaniqua. Ever since she returned to the ice cream shop, business has picked up there. Everyone loves the new bimbo version of her. And no one loves the new her more than she does. She began stopping into Blossom House regularly, partly to see Zella, but also to thank me.

But when it came to bimbofying the mayor again, I decided to do it in conjunction with the rest of her staff. Kitty was a real asset with this. A few people in the mayor's office had less than ideal reactions to her bimbo conversion, but overall, her upbeat and ditzy attitude went over really well.

And Kitty proved to be a great informant about the goings on in the office. She was a pipeline of information I was not supposed to be privy to. She basically gave me access to the entire email system within the mayor's office.

Kitty also gave me the lowdown on the marital problems the Harvests were having. As you may recall, Jacob Harvest had become upset that his wife started demanding a balanced relationship again. Those issues continued to the point where Danielle was sleeping in the guest bedroom. Jacob refused to share a bed with her.

I know that Danielle had started exploring the idea of divorce. Although I made sure her exploration didn't get very far. I arranged for all the lawyers in Blossom to turn down her request to represent her. With her mayoral duties, she had not had a chance to begin looking for a lawyer off-island. Of course, once her bimbofication complete again, she would be devoted to her husband and would be unable to even think of leaving him.

The Blossom Mayor's office holds a monthly staff meeting that everyone is required to attend. Usually they hold these meetings in a large meeting room onsite. Using Kitty as a go-between, I arranged for the next meeting to take place at Blossom House. It seemed easy enough for Kitty to convince the powers that be. I, of course, offered the full services of Blossom House for their meeting. It was the least I could do.

The mayoral office staff came over en masse, headed by Mayor Harvest herself. It was only a couple blocks, so they walked over.

As soon as my guests arrived, I found a reason for the mayor to be separated from her staff. I used the excuse of asking her to choose from the catering menu what would be served. Not that she ever got to see the menu. That was just the excuse to whisk Danielle away so that by the end of the meeting I could introduce her as Dani.

The whole process of hosting the staff meeting was complex. While I had the mayor's bimbofication process going in the back, I had a room full of people who needed to be bimbofied too.

Once again, I left the mayor in the talented hands of Jasmine and Violet. I also added Madison to the mix as a helping hand. The three girls had specific instructions on everything they were to do to the mayor, all written out in triplicate. There were three of them, after all.

With the main room, I started by plying everyone with food and drink. No one had any qualms about drinking wine at the staff meeting. And the crab cakes were a big hit.

Of course, the food and drinks were spiked with a special

chemical that would act as a catalyst. Everyone got dosed. Over time in the coming weeks, each person would experience changes in their bodies and personalities.

And from there, I went around adding extra touches to various people. Kitty was a big help once again, as she made suggestions for different people, depending on their background and role at work.

Obviously, the mayor's office is not completely staffed by women, although there are a large number of women working in her administration. But the men were changed too.

All the women would see changes to their bodies and their minds as the weeks wore on. That meant larger breasts and asses, thinner waists. It also meant a greater bimbo attitude with each passing day. After several months, they would be simple and happy. The boost to their libido would be very noticeable.

As for the men, they would find themselves with greater stamina and a penchant for asserting their dominance. They would also find it easier to maintain a healthy lifestyle and stay fit. I have never understood how men can expect to have a bombshell bimbo on their arms without putting in nearly as much work on their own appearance.

As Kitty and I moved around the room, I made changes to various people. Some women got physical boosts, bigger tits or a more shapely ass. Others gained a new appreciation for specific kinks. One woman, who already looked quite nice in her pre-bimbo form, suddenly found herself deeply attracted to Kitty. I figured she earned a reward for all of her help. I imagined the two of them would sneak off during breaks for a little extracurricular fun. Or they could just be shopping buddies. I wasn't going to pry.

The "staff meeting" which was really more of a party lasted for a full two hours without anyone asking questions.

Everyone was having too much fun. The inhibitions in the room had been dropped to near zero. It was great seeing so many people sharing themselves with each other. While there was sexual tension floating in the air, I was most impressed by how everyone seemed too finally open up with each other on a social and emotional level. That is the kind of healthy workplace I figured the Mayor's Office needed.

When Dani was finally ready to make her appearance, I met her first in the back. She looked perfect standing there in her new mayoral outfit. Sure, no one would expect her to make hard decisions, but that was what Jacob Harvest was there for. He would take over the actual work of Mayor and Dani would be the figurehead.

Seeing the fully bimbofied mayor for the first time told me I had made the right choice in coming to Blossom. She stood there in her pink platform high heeled shoes, wearing a tiny pink miniskirt and a white fitted blouse that barely contained her large breasts. The top buttons of her blouse were undone, showing off the entirety of her cleavage, making it clear she was not wearing a bra. Not that she could have closed those buttons. Her boobs were simply too big.

Dani's face had gone through a dramatic transformation: big eyes, small nose, plump lips, and an expression that made it clear nothing really happened inside her head. Like before her eye lashes were made permanently longer so as to better frame her blue eyes. Her hair now hung in long platinum blonde waves down to the small of her back, framing her face and forever leaving her the subject of dumb blonde jokes.

Then again, the jokes would now fit the bill. Most of her mind had been washed away, leaving behind a bubbly personality that wasn't much use except for looking pretty performing symbolic acts as mayor. And fucking. She was plenty good at that. Jacob would very much enjoy his wife's new proclivities toward sex.

I decided to make a big show of Dani's debut to her staff. I had also arranged for Jacob to drop by. I wanted him to see his new wife in all her glory.

I made the announcement. As the music played Mayor Dani Harvest walked out on stage to cheers and applause. She wore a beaming smile as she sashayed out on stage, using her new assets to best effect as she waved to her staff. She looked every bit a bimbo mayor. The first bimbo mayor the town of Blossom had ever had. And this time I knew it would stick.

After the song finished playing, Dani stepped down off the stage and into the waiting arms of her husband. She wrapped her in his strong arms and kissed her with a passion they had never dared show publicly. He knew she was his bimbo and he didn't care who knew it.

The party went on for another two hours. Mayor Dani, as she now preferred to be called, moved around the room, mostly hanging on her husband's arm, chatting with her staff. She was a big hit with everyone. Sure, no actual work was completed in the four-hour staff meeting, but no one, especially the mayor, seemed to mind.

As the party broke up, I sat back, tired from all of my work, but satisfied that I finally had Blossom back on track. With the mayor's office moving rapidly toward full bimbodom, it was only a matter of time before I had bimbofied the entire town.

14

BLOSSOM'S PINK HAT SOCIETY

It is easy to get distracted by young bimbos. Of the full bimbos I have created thus far in Blossom, nearly all of them have been in their twenties.

All of my girls are young and nubile. Of the other women I have completed full bimboizations on, only Mayor Dani is older, and she is admittedly pretty young for her role in Blossom.

When I bimbofy a town, I bimbofy everyone. I could see where only people of a certain age are bimbofied. Some bimbofiers are that way, although I am not. When I bimbofy a town, every one of legal age is bimbofied.

However, the simple fact is Blossom has a high number of older people. With Blossom being such a nice little town on a beautiful island, there are a large number of people who choose to retire here.

The large number of, quite frankly, senior citizens in Blossom poses an interesting conundrum. Again, many bimbofiers might regress everyone's ages to fit into the classic bimbo mold. The men and women who were once in retirement suddenly find themselves once again in their twenties and doing nothing but partying as they blow through their retirement savings.

I will say right now that age regression isn't my solution to the senior situation.

That obviously begs the question of what my solution is. For me, it is quite simple, age has no affect on whether a woman is a bimbo or not.

My plans with the senior population of Blossom come two fold. The men will be encouraged to join the same social groups as the younger men on the island. The women, however, will find themselves wanting to join a group I created called the Pink Hat Society.

You may have heard of the Red Hat Society. It is a women's group with chapters all across the country. The Pink Hat Society is similar, but with the intention of encouraging bimbo behaviors of its members.

I first planted the seeds of the group with several of the more prominent older women in Blossom around the same time my problems with the mayor first arose. I made Blossom House available to the group to meet and I suggested that they always wear pink hats to identify themselves. I made sure to provide hats.

Since then, I had mainly left the group to themselves. With the mayoral issues I was having, I didn't have time to give the Pink Hat Society much thought. To my great surprise, the group is quickly becoming just what I had hoped from them.

From the original five Pink Hat Society members, the group has now grown to over twenty with more women showing up for the meetings every week. That right there is impressive. And now that the group has become so popular, it is time to start truly bimbofying them.

The mind is the key with the senior bimbo. Where once

these women might have chatted about politics, they focus on gossip. While the talk of who is fucking whom was common, but always as a source of scandal, now it is both common and considered happy gossip.

Style and fashion also grow as a topic of conversation. After all, what woman doesn't want to look her best, especially when she is on the bimbo spectrum. And quite simply, the more the women attend Pink Hat Society meetings, the less intelligent they will seem. Even senior bimbos can be dumb.

Of course, I have physical changes planned too. First and foremost, the women of the PHS will find themselves gaining a level of fitness as if they had spent their entire lives working hard to stay fit. That right there will be enough to make many appear younger.

And then there are the changes to skin, lips, breasts and asses. Even though I am not trying to make these women look like they are in their twenties, they can still be rewarded with more bimbo-like features. Slight improvements of the skin will remove a few wrinkles and crows feet, fitting with their more health conscious image. Giving them more in the asset department certainly will add to the overall bimbo image. I might not go quite as large in the tits department, but no one will be complaining about the size and perkiness of her boobs.

Most importantly, the PHS ladies will be horny little minxes. For those who are married, their husbands will be quite happy. Especially since all the men in Blossom are being given greater stamina and control when it comes to sex. For those who are not married or are widows, there are plenty of eligible bachelors in their age group. Or they can seduce younger men if they please. There is no reason they can't be cougars too.

Blossom is well on its way to having a great community

of senior citizen bimbos and I couldn't be prouder. To be honest, I could see the Pink Hat Society spreading across the country, spreading the benefits of bimbodom.

15

THE CHANGING FASHIONS IN BLOSSOM

At a certain point, a town undergoing bimbofication will begin to see changes in the economy. One of the first places this becomes obvious is in clothing and accessory retail.

This should make sense when you think about it. The women in town develop new interests in fashion. And what's more, their changing bodies require them to go shopping, thus accelerating the change on local businesses.

I will be the first to say that Blossom is no Bimboville. The majority of the women in town would fit in on any street corner in America. Sure, the women of Blossom might be a little more stacked than average, but most of the women don't look like bimbos yet.

Still, the market for bras in Blossom has been the first part of the economy to change. First and foremost, the increase in breast size for the majority of women in Blossom has forced them all to buy new bras. The stores that did sell bras have had to send the small-cupped bras back to the manufacturer and replace them with much larger sizes.

The bra styles have changed too. It seems the more functional a bra appears, the less well it sells. Not only are women now preferring what I would call sexier bras, they are also buying ones that allow large amounts of cleavage to be shown.

I planned for a great deal of this from the beginning. I reached out to retailers, offering to connect them with new manufacturers and distributors who could meet the changing demands of the customers.

Additionally, I have helped arrange for clothing donations to women who cannot afford to keep up with the growing demands of their bodies. They should not be financially punished for my decision to bimbofy everyone in town.

While bras are the most obvious change, as every woman in town has experienced some growth in the breast department, other trends are appearing as well.

What many people would consider to be granny panties are no longer sold in Blossom. There is no one to buy them. Even the actual grannies, nearly all of them members of the Pink Hat Society, have switched to sexier styles.

Thongs are probably the most common form of panties worn these days in Blossom. Small bikini styles are next. That is assuming a woman decides to wear panties. From the rumors I have heard out of the Mayor's Office, Mayor Dani rarely wears anything beneath her short skirts. But with her husband now unofficially running the town's affairs, he is there to frequently bend her over and fuck what are left of her brains out. It only makes sense, from her perspective, to not bother with panties when they only seem to get in the way.

Beyond what I would term lingerie, there have also been subtle changes to the fashions worn in Blossom. Blossom itself is not a year-round tropical paradise. It gets cold in the winter. It rains, it snows. Women's fashion cannot just be skimpy, barely there strips of cloth that someone has decided to call clothing. There needs to be some function to it.

However, despite that fact, the popular styles in Blossom have been shifting toward being skimpier. Tops are tighter and they expose more cleavage. To be honest, I can't remember the last time I saw a turtleneck on a woman here.

Of course, the warmer weather has been helpful. I am seeing more shorts and skirts, both of which are much shorter than normal for Blossom, I think. I am also seeing more cropped tops, women showing off their tightening midriffs.

There has also been a run on shoes. The one shoe store in town is basically sold out of anything with a heel. The owner has more on order, but in the meantime, the residents are either digging into the backs of their closets for old pairs or they are ordering online.

What is funny was even the women who have been the least affected by my work thus far are also making changes to their wardrobes. I largely kept my distance from the local churches. The time to make my move on the religious institutions could come later, if needed.

However, I noticed the preacher's wife one day walking down the street. That in and of itself was nothing noteworthy. But seeing her wiggle down the street in a short sundress and tall wedge-heeled sandals made me smile. It was as if she had simply adopted the new look that many of the women around town were wearing without even thinking about it. I saw more of her that day than I had any other time I had met her.

At this stage, we had not reached total bimbo fashion, but I definitely enjoyed seeing progress toward that end being made.

16

A CONCERNED HUSBAND IN BLOSSOM

It was bound to happen eventually. We had our first concerned husband in Blossom.

It is actually surprising how few concerned spouses I run into in my line of work. I guess men really do prefer bimbos when it comes down to it. Of course, when I do mass bimbofications like I am with Blossom, I prep the men. Still, sometimes someone slips through the cracks.

That happened with a man named Richard Thorndike. Richard lives with his wife, Linda, in a cute little cottage with a water view. He primarily works off-island, commuting each day on the ferry. Linda thinks of herself as an author, although she has not had anything published in several years. She is an otherwise stay-at-home wife.

With Richard off-island so much, I guess he did not get to see much of his wife for a while. It only took him a couple months to figure out that his wife is changing.

I should mention that I am always a little surprised when concerned husbands seek me out for advice with their wives. In Blossom, I am simply known as the owner of Blossom House. Although I do try to maintain a positive presence in the community, I would not say that I am naturally someone people would come to for advice.

Still, Richard approaching me about Linda did not make him the first concerned husband to ask me for advice. Maybe deep down they know, even if they refuse to believe it, that I am ultimately responsible. I doubt it, but it would explain a lot. It could also just be the fact that I make myself appear trustworthy and that I am new to town.

Regardless as to why I always seem to be sought out, I do enjoy these moments with concerned spouses. I should note that women have come to me asking about why their husbands are treating them like they're stupid bimbos. Occasionally, the women did not realize they really were stupid bimbos.

Richard flagged me down as I pulled up to Blossom House for the evening shift. I don't spend all day at Blossom House, as I try to have a presence in town. And I do need my personal time as well.

As I got out of my car, Richard looked at me nervously. I could tell he had something to say, but he seemed to doubt himself. I would have wagered that there was a part of him that thought he was going crazy. I had seen the look before.

"Can I talk to you?" Richard asked. His nervousness nearly made him stutter.

"Sure," I said. "Why don't you come in and we can chat?"

Truthfully, I did not know what Richard wanted to talk about at that moment, but I could see that he had a serious concern to discuss with me.

"Yeah, okay," he said as I led him inside Blossom House. "It's about my wife, Linda, you see."

Up until that point I had figured I would bring him back to my office, but as soon as he mentioned his wife, I knew what this was about. Instead of going to my office, I arranged for use to sit in the main restaurant/lounge area. There's a particular table that gives a fantastic view of the rest of the room.

Normally I would have sat with my back to the wall so that I could survey my domain. However, with Richard I opted to give him that view.

Usually a concerned husband comes to me for one of two reasons. He is either struggling to see the benefits of his wife being a bimbo or he is faced with how to replace her income.

I collected a lot of data about all of the residents of Blossom. Yes, I know that sounds a bit like Big Brother, but it is helpful to know as much as I can about the people I am bimbofying. Now I can't keep every Blossom resident's information in my head, but I do memorize the list of women who either hold important roles in town or in their families. In this case, I knew Linda Thorndike was not on that list.

With that in mind, I already had Richard pegged as a man struggling to see the benefit of being married to a bimbo. And as such, I wanted him to have a view of the bimbos in Blossom House, whether they be my girls or patrons.

Before I let Richard continue, I called Ella over and ordered drinks for the two of us. I chose Ella specifically because she was the head bimbo of my girls. And she looked her bimbo best, wearing a tight little pink skirt and a tight white halter top that did little to contain her tits and left much of her midriff bare. She was prancing around in heels high enough to give most women vertigo. But not Ella. She lived in heels now, like all my girls.

Richard's eyes bugged out as seeing Ella. She giggled when she noticed Richard staring. Personally, I couldn't help but notice Ella had gotten her nose pierced. That wasn't a change I created. She chose to do it. And it looked good. It fit her look and gave people something to look at when they weren't looking at her tits, her ass, or her tight midriff. Not that Ella needed a reason. She was a bimbo after all.

It was not until Ella returned with our drinks that I let Richard continue. He took a long drink of his beer. His shoulders relaxed. He was finally ready to talk.

And it was exactly what I had figured. I will spare you a recitation of what he said, but it seemed that he was struggling with Linda's new attitudes and behaviors.

It was as if Richard suddenly woke up to the changes in his wife. Now most of that could be explained by him working long hours that kept him away from home. He even stayed at a hotel a few nights because he missed the final ferry of the day.

It was not until he got a week off that he suddenly realized the woman he married was different now. She seemed more sexual and far less interested in writing. In fact, Richard probed her and she finally admitted she hadn't even turned on her computer in three weeks.

Richard did admit they had a lot of sex in that week. But once the week was over, he started to question what had happened to Linda. And for some reason that even Richard was unsure as to why, he sought me out.

I have always wondered how best to lead a man to water. Or in this case, how to lead him to an appreciation of bimbos. I imagine it is a lot like teachers figuring out the best methods to test their students. There are many ways to do it, but which way is best?

With Richard, and I will admit with most concerned husbands, I took the position of using a combination of logic and demonstration. But before I laid down my logic, I sympathized with Richard. He needed to know that he wasn't going crazy. I find sympathy among humans to be both a powerful thing and something that far too few people use. I may bimbofy people against their will, but I will at least treat them with dignity.

As I spoke, showing sympathy with his issue, I could tell

Richard's eyes were tracking the waitresses. I couldn't blame him. My girls are all quite breathtaking. And their sex appeal was definitely having an effect on Richard.

"Have you enjoyed the last week?" I asked, already knowing what the answer would be. Richard nodded his head, almost afraid to actually boast about the great sex he had all week.

"Would you like to always have sex like that?" I continued. Again, he nodded his head.

I already knew I had him. From there is was easy too lead him down the path to preferring bimbos. In the end, I really think most men would prefer being with a bimbo. Many just don't know it yet.

Once Richard seemed more keen on the idea of Linda being a bimbo, I called over Zella. She didn't bounce around as much as the other girls. That wasn't her style. She was the bad girl of the bunch after all. Not that she did anything bad. She just liked making people think she did.

As Zella stood there, I asked Richard what kind of woman he wanted Linda to be, if he could have his deepest desire. I used Zella as an example, showing her off. I could tell she liked it. Her breathing grew heavier. She was getting horny.

It did not take long for Richard to start spilling his desires. I think it helped to give him a comparison between Ella and Zella. I think he liked the forwardness of Zella, because she was very clear about her intentions, but I think he liked the classic look of Ella.

"Are you feeling better about Linda now?" I asked after I had dismissed Zella. I told her to go on break. She needed some release, which for her could mean either sucking or fucking. That was just how she rolled.

"I really am," Richard answered. "I guess I hadn't thought about it from all the angles."

"I understand," I said. "And you've been working hard. It's only fair that Linda helps you relax when you're not working."

"You're absolutely right. But there's still something I don't get."

"Why?" I posed, knowing what his question would be.

"Yeah."

"Why question such a gift? I am sure you and Linda will be very happy together. You should enjoy life and not worry so much."

It is interesting how sometimes bimbo advice works for non-bimbos too. Once Richard stopped worrying so much, I was sure his happiness would go through the roof.

As I showed Richard out, I started formulating what I wanted to do with Mrs. Thorndike the next time I saw her. I had already decided to give her the tits she deserved. She could stand to have longer and blonder hair too. Richard liked the classic bimbo look and I was going to give it to him. And Linda, she would be happy regardless.

GIVING LINDA THORNDIKE THE
FULL BIMBO TREATMENT

After my discussion with Richard Thorndike, I decided finish Linda Thorndike's bimbofication ahead of schedule. I had planned to guide her overall transformation, but let it happen at the normal pace as the rest of the town.

However, I decided to go ahead with it and make both Linda and Richard happier. The sooner Linda ass able to give herself to her new role in the life, the better it would be for everyone, I figured.

It started with a special invitation to Blossom House.

Linda arrived, already looking quite fetching, I thought. She wore one of the new bras I had helped bring into town, in a size that she had never needed before I set up shop.

But other than her increased bust size, she did not look all that different than she probably did before I started bimbofying the town. She certainly had not updated her wardrobe any. She wore a skirt, but it was a long flowing skirt that concealed rather than highlighted her body. Her top was simple and did nothing to highlight her new assets either.

That, of course, would change shortly.

Linda Thorndike had no idea what she was in for when she arrived at Blossom House. She showed the invitation at the door and she was quickly ushered to the small onsite gym we have.

I should mention that I have decided to partner with the local gym. They have the capacity to handle a growing number of townspeople working out and it means I can use the extra square footage toward other purposes.

Despite that, it is still important to maintain an onsite gym, even if it cannot handle more than a few people working out at once.

Linda first met with Madison. I have not mentioned her much thus far, other than to explain where she came from. She is the fitness and sporty bimbo of my girls.

The plan with Linda was surprisingly simple. First, she would work out with Madison, working up a good sweat and activating her metabolism. Madison would also be preparing a bimbo workout regimen for Linda to help her keep the body she would be leaving with. It's important to maintain gains, even if those gains did not come from workouts themselves.

Linda had not been prepared for a workout, but I keep everything needed in stock. She was a little self-conscious about just wearing a sports bra, spandex shorts and workout shoes, but with Madison's encouragement, she jumped right in.

One of the important bimbo exercises are squats. The ass is an often overlooked aspect in the development of the bimbo. So often people get caught up on the tits. Don't get me wrong, big tits are great, but they don't make the bimbo. The bimbo is the whole package.

Madison worked Linda hard, walking her through her new workout routine. It was better to teach Linda how to do the exercises before her mind had been turned to bimbo mush so that she could actually retain it.

After Linda's workout, she took a shower and then visited Jasmine for a nice and relaxing massage. At this point, Linda was in no state to worry about being naked in front of Jasmine. She would find that and certain other inhibitions would worry her no more.

The massage did two things. One, the oils Jasmine used worked to slow Linda's mind. I sometimes feel bad about lowering the IQ's of people, but I know the new Linda will be much happier without the extra brain matter getting in the way.

The oils will also make several substantial improvements to Linda's body. Her skin will be perfected, her breasts grown to a size where the bra she walked in with will have no hope of containing them, and her lower legs will adapt to more feminine footwear.

Linda's blissful smile is all I need to see when she makes her way to see Violet in the salon. Violet has become an important cog in my bimbofication machine. She not only is good at what she does, but she has gained my trust in her bimbo aesthetic. I trust her to call audibles when they are needed, unless, of course, she is under strict guidance for a specific look.

In the case of Linda, I told Violet that we are looking for a classic look. She then knows what constraints she is under.

Violet begins by washing Linda's hair. The shampoo acts more like hair dye in that it changes the subject's hair color. But instead of temporarily dyeing the hair, it changes the color her hair will grow. And thus, in short order, Linda was given a beautiful shade of bleach blonde hair, the kind normally you would need to get from a bottle, but for her, it will grow that way naturally from now on.

Once Linda had a new color and hairstyle, Violet moved on to makeup. It takes time to find the right palette to work from. But two things that Linda got, regardless of the final color palette, was a limp plumping lipstick and eyelash lengthening mascara. The lipstick is especially important to create the plump pillows that Linda will need to better suck Richard's cock. One coating is usually enough for most people, although I have had requests for second coats occasionally.

While Violet worked, I made a few changes to Linda's mind. If anyone met Linda now, they would know instantly that she was a bimbo. She would come across as another dumb blonde, something Blossom is becoming known for. But Richard liked the assertiveness of Zella, so I increased Linda's assertiveness, at least when it came to things like style and her desire for sex. I doubted Richard would ever need to instigate sex again, although, like any man, he probably still would on occasion.

When it came time to help Linda select a new outfit, she was in a much better position to actually contribute. It did not take long for Linda to pass on wearing a two-piece outfit. She only had eyes for dresses.

And of the dresses Linda now eyed, none of them would have been something she would have been caught wearing before. After trying on multiple dresses, taking more than an hour to select the perfect one, Linda walked out of Blossom House wearing a short red dress with multiple cutouts and sides that laced together, helping to reveal the fact she was wearing neither a bra nor panties.

Linda paired the dress with black high heels with a sole that matched the dress. Considering she had never been a big fan of heels before, walking out of Blossom House, she was a natural. Of course, her heels would never again touch the ground when she was walking. She would walk on her toes when barefoot.

Before Linda left, she thanked me and my girls for helping her. She said she felt better than ever. Her next goal was to seduce her husband the moment he got home from work. Her only problem, she admitted, was not knowing if she should suck him off, or get him to fuck either her pussy or ass instead. And those options didn't include a titfuck. Bimbos have the hardest choices to make sometimes.

No matter how the Thorndike's celebrated their new reality, everyone was the happier for Linda's bimbofication.

18

BIMBO ICE CREAM IN BLOSSOM

I decided to pay a visit to Shaniqua at the ice cream shop by the ferry landing. It was a warm day and I felt like having an ice cream cone. And who wouldn't want to be served by the best bimbo ice cream girl in town?

When Shaniqua spotted me, her face lit up with a big smile. She definitely seemed happy with her new life. She might not be college material anymore, but I was pretty sure she didn't care. I doubted she even realized she had her degree at this point.

One thing I noticed from the moment I walked into the little shop was the overt sluttiness of all three women working behind the counter. First off, Shaniqua had adopted a much more revealing outfit than the one she had originally been given for work. She wore a skimpy pink halter top that left much of her tits and midriff on display and a tiny pair of cutoff jean shorts that looked almost painted onto her ass.

The other two women were not so bold, but they definitely were pushing the boundaries of what I would have expected to be acceptable by their boss. The other two women wore low cut cropped t-shirts and short jean shorts, but they were not nearly as risqué as Shaniqua's outfit.

At first glance, I could not tell if the slutty dress of the ice cream shop employees was out of jealousy of Shaniqua or from the general shift among the people of Blossom. Just walking down the street, one can see the change in how women are dressed, but these two other women were definitely more provocatively dressed than the norm in town.

"What can I, like, get for you?" Shaniqua asked when it was my turn to order.

"Hmm, what's your favorite flavor?" I asked.

Shaniqua stood there looking at me and trying to think. I always enjoyed watching bimbos think. They could be so adorable. In Shaniqua's case, she stuck her tongue out slightly and nearly crossed her eyes as she attempted to first remember what the flavors were and then recall which one she liked best.

After about two minutes of this, I figured Shaniqua forgot she was trying to answer a question. I just laughed.

"I'll have a sugar cone with chocolate fudge," I said, making my order.

Shaniqua seemed relieved to have something else to do and jumped about in her high heels as she prepared my order. Seeing her mince about was also quite adorable. The other women, I noticed, were not wearing heels. I could tell by the way they moved around.

The way Shaniqua bent at the waist when making my cone, I could tell she did so to give me, and anyone else who might be watching, a good look at her tits. It also gave her coworkers a great view of her ass.

"There you, like, go," Shaniqua said as she handed me my cone. She had a bigger smile than ever. I think she really liked serving ice cream. Of course, the cold from the freezers had a definite effect on her nipples. They were hard little bullets poking out against her top.

Shaniqua continued to pose while one of her coworkers rang up my purchase. I had no doubt that Shaniqua could not longer work the register. Her ability to work with numbers in any significant manner was shot. She was all bimbo bubbliness with an extra helping of sexy now.

I wished the three ladies a nice day before I stepped back out into the sunshine with my ice cream cone in hand. I could hear the giggles behind me as I decided to make my way toward Blossom House. After checking in with Shaniqua, I figured it would be good to check in with my girls.

19

THE FINAL STAGE OF THE BLOSSOM HOUSE GIRLS

I very much enjoyed my walk back to Blossom House. The walk was uphill, away from the water, but the ice cream more than made up for it.

The moment I walked in the door, it was Ella who rushed over to greet me, wanting to see if there was anything I needed. One of the things that makes her so good at her job is how attentive she can be. And it is not only with me, but with all of the patrons that she does this with.

She creates so many smiles from people as soon as they walk in the door. Her own beaming smile is a big part of that. So too is her generous display of cleavage.

Ella has been on a big fitness kick recently. She comes in early to work with Madison. Of course, with my talents, I have helped Ella along on her fitness journey. Her current goal is to get a six pack. She is well on her way.

To be honest, I think her working on her abs was half the reason she got her belly-button pierced. Just another reason to highlight a great feature. She has definitely been showing her midriff off as much as possible with the way she has been dressing, however. I can't remember the last time she wore an outfit that didn't show off her belly-button.

If Ella has become the primary greeter at Blossom House, it is Raven who usually sees most of the guests next. Waiting for a table? Go join Raven at the bar. She'll pour you a delicious drink and flirt with you until your table is ready.

Raven has continued to evolve. She started out as a goth by default. Now no one would ever know she once wore even the smallest hint of black. She has really played up her femininity. For a bar tender, she could never be mistaken for one of the boys.

To emphasize her femininity, Raven has adopted certain behaviors and styles. When it comes to her clothing, she only ever wears skirts. There are no exceptions in that.

She acts in a very specific way too. Yes, she flirts with everyone. But it's more than her constant flirting with the men and women visitors. The simplest way to describe her is high maintenance. While she mixes a great drink, she can be a little slow about it. Raven is fastidious when it comes to keeping her appearance in top shape, including her long nails. And she works hard to keep a spotless bar. One spilled drop is too many.

In contrast, Brittney is awful with details like that. She is so easily distracted. Her attention can be snagged by the smallest things. Sometimes all it takes is a light reflection to distract her and leave her staring off into nothing.

I actually think Brittney is willfully making herself more dumb. It certainly has not been anything I've done to her. At this point, we mostly use her to take food and drinks to customers, since her memory is basically shot at this point. I'm not even sure she is able to form long term memories at this point. She lives as if she is floating from one moment to the next. I've taken to programming her phone to tell her what to do and when. Otherwise, she would never make it into work.

Nancy spends much less time in the kitchen now. She has started belly dancing throughout the dinner hour as a form of entertainment. I am thinking of eventually putting on a weekend variety show which will heavily feature Nancy's dancing. The final version will probably need to wait until the whole town has been bimbofied. Not everyone would accept a show called the Bimbo Hour, or something like that. The bimbos I have already created in town might identify with the name, but not enough people have passed the point of no return yet.

Physically, Nancy has actually grown more flexible. The way she can contort her body is phenomenal. And remember, she isn't one of those flat chested girls anymore. Nancy has some serious curves. She could make any leotard appear pornographic, if she chose.

Abigail has taken the school girl act to an extreme. She is constantly listening to pop music and dancing around the kitchen as she cooks. Her short tartan skirts are constantly swishing about her, frequently revealing her panties.

Outside of the kitchen, Abigail has a little teddy bear backpack that she carries a couple books in. However, rather than school appropriate books, she prefers titles such as "How to Suck Cock." When she pulls the books out to peruse, she definitely does so with a smirk. Lucky for her, the books she chooses have lots of pictures, because her reading level has fallen precipitously since she joined Blossom House.

Someone who needs no lessons on sucking cock is Zella. She has become quite the pro. And using her bad girl image, she has found a way to suck every cock on the police force, except her father's of course. Zella uses a made up offense to give her reason to suck the cop's cock. To be honest, I think she really believes she is getting away with something.

Zella has also found new ways to play up her bad girl reputation. Following Ella's decision to get her belly button pierced, Zella has made several trips to the piercing parlor. After each trip, she has informed me about what work she has had done. Some is obvious, including her belly button and multiple piercings in her ears. She also has dermal piercings in the small of her back. I suppose she chose those over a tattoo. Less obvious are the pierced nipples and pierced clit.

But the one she is most proud of is her pierced tongue. And with my help, the healing time was nearly instantaneous. We can't have Zella falling out of practice or denying the many men in Blossom the use of her talented mouth.

I should not leave out my three other girls. They may have joined Blossom House later than their peers, but they arrived fully bimbofied. Nonetheless, they have continued on their own bimbo journeys.

Madison has been a great help in encouraging the fitness of the Blossom House patrons. She is an excellent motivator. And soon she will be starting a sex exercise class. It will be specifically designed for women to build sexual strength and stamina.

And speaking of sex, Jasmine, the Blossom House masseuse, has been given the okay to give the occasional happy ending to her massages. She has full discretion on who will be given such honors and she is not to accept money or tips for the bonus. Jasmine seems much happier now.

That just leaves Violet. She has become instrumental in the bimbo transformation work we do at Blossom House. I've actually been keeping close tabs on her, because she has not seemed as happy as I figured she would. She takes her job very seriously. Too seriously for a bimbo. I'm on the lookout for someone who likes her look and can fuck her on the regular. I think that's what she really needs. I'll find her someone eventually.

That's about it for my girls right now. The bimbofication of Blossom is a constantly evolving process.

THE MAYOR'S OFFICE IS BIMBO CENTRAL IN BLOSSOM

With Mayor Dani fully bimbofied, I had found myself not stopping in at the Mayor's Office as often. In fact, it had been quite a while since I last stopped in. Basically, if I didn't have business there, I didn't go. And I haven't had recent business at the Mayor's Office.

This trip was purely a social call. I will fully admit I had no specific business with the mayor or her office. I simply wanted to check in with how everything was going.

Not that Kitty would ever question my presence in the Mayor's Office. Her face lights up every time she sees me. Admittedly, she is usually happy to see almost anyone, but she always seems especially happy to see me.

Despite the office being busy, Kitty took the time to catch me up on all the goings on. As I suspected would happen, Jacob Harvest has taken over most of the decision making for his wife.

Mayor Dani, as she now prefers to be called, even by her husband, is mostly just a figurehead for Blossom. She attends events, always looking her bimbo best. If she makes a speech, it is always short. Her husband keeps her from babbling too much. And babbling is what she tends to do a lot of when under pressure to speak. It's quite funny, really.

However, as soon as I walked in, I could sense there was a major difference in the office culture. The women were all dressed to show off. And they had plenty to show off. At Dani's coming out party, I bimbofied almost all of the staff to some degree. And over the following weeks, that bimbofication continued.

The Mayor's Office remains a professional workplace, but that does not mean the women don't display themselves to great effect. And as far as I can tell, everyone still takes their jobs seriously, even if it is now commonplace to find yourself looking into a deep valley of cleavage or at a nice round ass in an impossibly tight skirt. It has become the new normal.

And I have little doubt that the amount of flirting in the office has gone way up. The sexual tension in the building is much higher than it was before. Yet, I can tell that the employees are not taking breaks together, if you know what I mean. Yes, some of the more libidinous women do need regular bathroom breaks to maintain their composure, but they are not dragging men into closets to satisfy their carnal urges.

However, it is not just clothing styles and libidos that have changed. The women in the office are now much more deferential toward the men. They are hesitant to make hard decisions and they take less initiative than they once did.

In one case, one of the town managers and her assistant, a man, completely switched places. He is now the manager and she is his assistant. They both seem much happier now.

With all this change, one might think that the Mayor's Office would be in turmoil, or would have experienced a massive loss in efficiency. If anything, the opposite has been true. The backlogs that had plagued certain departments have all but disappeared. The staff has actually gotten smaller, because the administrative bureaucracy has been cut. And even with all of that, employees are working less. They either leave early or take additional vacation days.

So as far as I can tell, the changes I have created in the Mayor's Office are enjoyed by all. The office is working better and more efficiently, everyone seems much happier, and I think most importantly, Mayor Dani and her employees are acting as great role models for the denizens of Blossom.

PUTTING BLOSSOM ON THE MAP

Blossom is a tourist town. It's hard not to be when the island is as close to paradise as possible, at least during the summer. Tourists from all over the world come and visit every year.

In general, I have kept the tourists free of the bimbofication process. Any that have been exposed have been exposed at such minor levels, it would not be noticeable long term. Or at least, not in any way that would cause concern. I guarantee no one would complain if a woman decided she suddenly showed an interest in oral sex, or if she finds herself looking just a little more attractive.

But word has started to spread about the attractiveness of Blossom women. I generally keep my eye out for journalists, but we had one slip through the cracks recently.

Penny Olson worked for a national investigative magazine. She came to town, posing as a tourist and snooping around, trying to answer the question of why were there so many bimbos in Blossom.

I should begin by saying that she did not use the word

bimbo to describe the residents of Blossom. But I must say, the name Penny does seem like a bimboish name.

Ms. Olson did a fantastic job of remaining under my radar. She had been here for a week before I started to hear rumors of a reporter sniffing around town. And yet, despite the rumors, I could not find her. Having a reporter looking into the bimbofication of Blossom was concerning. We bimbofiers do prefer to keep a low profile outside of the communities we bimbofy.

In the end, it came down to luck that Ms. Olson and I met face to face. She sought me out as an influential resident. She wanted to know if I had noticed anything strange.

I offered to meet Ms. Olson at Blossom House. It is my place of work, after all. She agreed, but the moment I saw her step inside, I could tell that she was beginning to understand that she had made a mistake. She got one look at Ella and she knew Blossom House was a bimbo hotbed.

I could have just done a full bimbofication on her right there. It would have been easy. And with the name of Penny, it seemed perfect. But I held back. The simple fact was, if Penny left Blossom as a complete bimbo, it would raise far too many red flags.

Instead, I took a more subtle approach. No, I could not let Ms. Olson write her article. And as it turned out, she had gathered quite a bit of data. Although she had nothing that led to me and she had thankfully not shared the information with anyone else, including her editor.

It was simple enough to wave her off the story. By the time she left, she would be convinced there was nothing of note going on in Blossom. She would also be calling her editor to share that belief with her bosses.

That solved the immediate problem. It took the heat off of me, Blossom House and Blossom in general. But there was no way I was going to let Penny Olson walk out of Blossom unchanged.

All it took was planting a seed in her mind. At first, nothing would happen. Ms. Olson would return to her old life as if nothing had happened to her. But slowly over time, she would find herself adopting behaviors and interests of a bimbo.

It would start as an increased libido. Then she would begin wanting to dress in a more sexy manner, her clothing tastes evolving over time. She would also begin to adopt certain speech patterns, probably something along the lines of a valley girl style of speech.

If you can't already tell, I'm not a fan of people getting into my business. Under normal circumstances, when I plant a bimbofication seed, I have their body adapt along with the mental changes. They get the body modifications for free.

But with Ms. Olson being on my bad list, I decided she deserved to pay for her upgrades herself, that is assuming she could not find a generous man to pay for them. Thus, all of the physical changes would need to come from hard work, and it would be hard work she chose to put in. Her desire to look and act like a stereotypical bimbo would become a compulsion. Soon, she would just be Penny the bimbo.

Don't think of me as cruel. Yes, I use the bimbofication as a punishment. But in the end, I know Penny the bimbo will be far happier than Penny Olson the investigative reporter, ever would be, even though she will no longer be able to work as a reporter.

My one regret about the interaction was I did not include a desire for her to contact me when her transformation was complete. I would love to see the final product. But at least I get to see plenty of finished products in Blossom.

BLOSSOM TATTOOS

Blossom House is expanding outside its walls. I have waited to reach this point, largely because I am personally not a fan. However, some people are and I must cater to others. For that reason, I opened a tattoo parlor.

As I said, tattoos are not my thing. I prefer to see unblemished skin on my bimbos. Admittedly, I may be in the minority, but I will accept that. Even if I'm not a fan of the end results, I can at least use the process for my benefit and enjoyment.

Blossom has long had a tattoo parlor, named simply Blossom Tattoo. Unfortunately, the owner has suffered some health issues and has decided to retire from actual work. That is the official story. Unofficially, she has retired to a life of sucking her husband's cock. My understanding is she is much happier now. So is her husband.

I couldn't leave the island completely devoid of its tattoo needs. That is why I quietly purchased the building and the business. Publicly I am helping keep local businesses alive. Privately, I am having a little fun.

The first step after acquiring the business was to find

someone to run it. I didn't care so much about financial side of it. If you think Blossom House is making me money, you would be mistaken. But when you have abilities and knowledge like I do, money tends not to be a major impediment. And it is simple enough to set up a basic point of sale system that even the simplest of bimbos can be trained to use.

There was no way I was going to cannibalize my current staff for this new venture. That meant finding someone new. As it turned out, a new resident to Blossom proved to be the perfect candidate.

Olivia was close to becoming a college dropout. Her parents had recently moved to Blossom. Her mother was already undergoing a low level of bimbofication. Olivia had thus far mostly evaded my net. However, that was largely because she spent most of her time during her semester off from school hiding out in her room, drawing in a notebook.

It was easy enough to get Olivia out of the house. A simple nudge from me had her parents demand she find work if she was going to live under their roof without going to school. She didn't have any skills when it came to tattoos, but that was easy enough to give her once I had otherwise ensnared her.

At her parents' urging, Olivia came to me asking if I knew of any available jobs. She didn't really know me, but my reputation in town was impeccable. That seemed to be enough for her. And of course, I did have a job.

Without going into details, I showed her where she would begin work as soon as she had been properly prepped and trained.

"You want me to work at a tattoo parlor?" Olivia asked when I showed her inside. "I don't even have a tattoo."

"But you secretly want one, don't you," I said, pushing that desire on to her.

"How did you know?" Olivia asked in surprise. "I've never told anyone that before."

"It's obvious the way you look at this place in awe," I answered, again pushing those new ideas on to her. She responded by a certain awe and reverence showing on her face as she looked around the small shop.

"What would I do here?" she asked. "I know nothing about tattoos."

"You don't have to worry about that," I said. "I know just how to get you started."

Despite my dislike of tattoos, I have long used it as a bimbofying method. I have a special ink that tends to make what is written on the body true.

"You do?" Olivia asked. She seemed a little bewildered. That was going to be a common feeling, although it would manifest itself differently soon.

"I do. And the first step is for you to take off your top and bra. Then I want you to lie face down on that table." I pointed toward a surface that looked much like a massage table.

I could see the hesitation in Olivia's movements. She had no reason to trust me. Yet it only took a small mental push on my part to override her fears. She would learn to trust me completely very soon.

It only took a few minutes for Olivia to fully comply with my request. Once she was face down on the table I brought out the special ink I use. Thankfully, this ink did not require any needles. I could simply draw with it on the skin and it would sink in becoming a permanent tattoo. I also had developed a benign version that could be used for regular tattooing, but I would not be using that version on Olivia.

"Are you ready for your first tattoo?" I asked.

Despite the fact we had never discussed what kind of tattoo she suddenly wanted, she nodded her head in affirmation. That was enough agreement for me to begin my work.

Since I wasn't using needles, I did not need to worry about pain. That left me more options with placement.

I chose to write vertically down Olivia's spine using a stylized font. I only needed five letters to start. B-I-M-B-O.

I took my time, wanting to make sure I got it right. It would be a baseline for everything else Olivia would get over time.

"Are you ready to see it?" I asked once I had finished. "Since it's on your back, I'll take a picture with your phone so you can see it better."

I picked up Olivia's phone and quickly snapped a picture. I then handed it to the waiting Olivia.

"Why did you write BIMBO?" Olivia asked. She was not mad, but she was confused.

"Because it's obvious to everyone how much of a bimbo you are."

"Oh yeah," Olivia said with a giggle. "I forgot. I'm such a bimbo sometimes."

"Not to worry," I said, chuckling. "Are you ready for another one?"

"Um, sure," she said.

"Let's flip you over for these next ones."

This time there was no hesitation. Olivia flipped onto her back, happy to do as she was told. The ink had already taken control of her mind.

This time in small script I wrote the words Big Tits & Ass just below and to the outside of her left breast along her ribs.

In short order Olivia developed just such attributes. Her small breasts expanded out into large melons that dominated her upper body. Her otherwise flat ass also ballooned out into an impressive size, although that was harder to see with her still wearing a pair of pants that now appeared painted onto her rear end.

If Olivia noticed the physical change in herself, she certainly did not show it.

I switched sides and wrote Dumb Blonde in the same position under her right breast. Any remaining intelligence seemed to fade from Olivia's eyes as her hair turned a bright shade of blonde. She was definitely starting to look the part.

With much of bimbo Olivia complete, there was only one thing I had left to do. She was a great bimbo, but she still needed some tattoo skills. Not wanting to ink her body in an obvious way, I used a micro applicator. I could draw on Olivia's skin in such a small area that it would appear as a dot on her skin at most.

I marked her body with several phrases that would give her the skills and confidence to become a fully capable tattoo artist, even if she was a bimbo in every other respect. And by the time I left her to her own devices, she had become a fully qualified tattooist, even understanding the safety and cleanliness required of her.

Of course, I allowed her to decorate her own body as she wished. She was to use the benign ink on herself and on customers, unless I said otherwise. After all, moving part of my operation outside of Blossom House did open me up to a certain amount of risk. Nonetheless, I believed it was a risk worth taking.

It took a couple days before word fully spread about the reopening of Blossom Tattoo and of the sexy bimbo tattoo artist that Olivia had become. In her free time she enjoyed herself, adding new tattoos. She asked me to help with a few pieces on her backside, which I was happy to help with. She was one of my girls now.

By the time business had truly picked up at Blossom Tattoo, Olivia had indulged herself quite a bit. She had thankfully kept her face and neck clean, but she had otherwise liberally decorated her body. She sported a pair of red lips on her ass, as well as a lower back tribal piece that screamed basic bimbo. She had also drawn a spiral design around her navel that pointed toward a piercing she had gotten.

Both her arms were covered in tattoo sleeves. Her left arm was covered in an array of geometric shapes that was probably inspired by one of her notebook drawings. Her right arm was covered in vines that wrapped around each other and her arm all the way down to her hand.

Overall, I liked how Olivia had kept her tattoos tasteful. There was one deviation, however. She wrote the words fuck and suck on her fingers, one letter on each finger. I very nearly removed it, something which I can do easily. However, I thought better of it. I even went back and drew over them with the special ink. Olivia was not just going to be a tattooed bimbo. She was going to be a tattooed bimbo slut. And she certainly became one.

Most of the time, Olivia uses the benign ink. However, there are times I request she use the special ink. When that happens, everyone seems to enjoy the outcome.

23

GIMBOS IN BLOSSOM

I tried to keep myself from bimbofying the tourists. It was impossible to keep them completely bimbo free, but I certainly didn't target them directly.

However, there were two women who passed through town, that I couldn't help but taking a liking to. They were an unusual pair. It wasn't often that you saw goths in Blossom, but there they were, perusing the local independent book store as I walked by on my way from the harbor up to Blossom House.

I began by making inquiries with the local hotels, wanting to find out where the two women were staying and, of course, learn their names. That was how I discovered they went by Winter and Flame.

Once I determined where they were staying, I offered the pair a special visit to Blossom House, through the hotel management. It was easy to convince them that it was a random drawing by the hotel and to keep my involvement out of it. After all, I prefer to play my games from behind the scenes. Of course, the hotel manager had me to thank for his bimbo wife playing to his every sexual need between cleaning the rooms as a bimbo maid. He owed me.

To my great delight, Winter and Flame made their appearance at Blossom House that night for dinner. My establishment might not be on the water, but the chance at a free meal was more than enough to attract anyone to my place of business. The "complete package" that I left undefined in their certificate was simply icing on the cake to them, I was sure.

I had reserved a special booth for the pair, someplace a little out of the way so the bimboness of Blossom House would not be on full display. Since Raven is no longer goth, I felt Zella was the best of my staff to wait on the pair. Her preference for leather would help endear her to them, or at least that was my hope. With bimbos, there are always unplanned incidents.

Winter came to Blossom House dressed for the season of her name with a long black leather coat. She wore it fully buttoned, revealing as little of her body as possible. She wore black combat boots and black lipstick. Her pale milky-white skin contrasted even more due to her jet black hair that flowed down over her shoulders and far down her back.

Flame also came to Blossom House wearing combat boots, but she appeared much more Victorian with a black and purple dress. She maintained the purple theme with purple lipstick. While Winter had long black hair, Flame wore hers short and spiked. Her face seemed to naturally have more color than her friend, but she hid it with thick white makeup.

For their opening drinks order, I played bartender, adding an extra ingredient that I was certain they would end up enjoying. I had been working on a temporary bimbocant, a tasteless liquid that would temporarily bimbofy the target's mind for a day or two. I hadn't worked out all the kinks, but I knew it worked and I knew it was temporary.

By the time Zella was delivering their food, they were both giggling like school girls. Zella even reported they complimented her tits. That told me they were definitely ready for the next stage.

After they finished their dinner, Zella invited them back to see me and Violet. When the two giggling goth girls entered the Blossom House wardrobe, I stood there with Violet at a special display I had set up for them.

"Are you enjoying yourselves?" I asked. I didn't get an actual answer, but between the giggling and the nodding, I got the answer I was looking for. "I am glad. As part of the complete package, you two get your fill of not only the large wardrobe we have here during your stay, but also these special potions. None of them are dangerous, but they do have some effects that I think both of you will enjoy. Try anything you like. And if you have questions, our resident stylist here is Violet. She knows the wardrobe better than anyone."

I took my leave and then retired to my office where I could watch what came next on closed circuit television, thankfully in full color.

"Tits?" Winter asked. "What do you think this one means?" She punctuated both questions with a further giggle. She then looked down at her body. It was hard to tell with her coat, but she did not look all that developed in the breast department.

Before either Violet could answer, Winter picked up the small bottle labeled Tits and drank it down. She then put it back in its place.

It only took a few moments before the potion went to work. "Ouchie," Winter cried out with her bimbofied vocabulary. However, even as a bimbo, she realized what was happening and what she needed to do to fix it.

Winter quickly began to strip, pulling off her coat and then the black clothing underneath it. By the time she was down to just her bra, her rapidly expanding tits were pushing up over the cups with red marks formed on her shoulders, her back and on the flesh of her still expanding breasts.

It was only with the help of both Violet and Flame that Winter was able to remove the offending bra and let her new assets breathe free air. They were big and heavy, but Winter loved them. She giggled, making them jiggle. The jiggling felt good and made her giggle all the more.

Flame, seeing what had happened to her friend, quickly put two and two together. She quickly started to strip out of her dress, getting fully naked and not caring a lick that she was standing nude before a stranger. Then she started looking through the potions.

Jealous of Winter, Flame found another potion. This one was labeled Fake Tits. Not wanting to be outdone by her friend, she focused on the Tits part and eagerly drank it down.

There was no pain for Flame as two round orbs grew out of her chest, giving her an unnaturally buoyant set of breasts that rivaled Winter's in size.

After that, the two women took turns altering their bodies with the potions provided. From there, it was a whirlwind tour of the wardrobe, with Violet finding just the right outfits to fit their bimbo desires.

When Winter and Flame returned to the main floor for one final drink that night, they looked very little like the goth girls they had once been. They were still very much goth. I had done nothing to change that. But they were now every bit the goth bimbos they appeared to be.

Winter still wore a long coat, but she left it open, letting it flow behind her like a cape. Underneath, she wore a black corset that pushed her tits up almost to her chin and left a narrow belt of pale skin above a black leather skirt and black fishnet stockings. Rather than the combat boots she entered wearing, Winter wore high heeled platform boots that reached her knees.

Flame wore what amounted to a pleasant blouse with a tied front that left her shoulders bare as well as gave a great view of her cleavage through the loosely tied front. The blouse also barely came down below her obviously fake tits, leaving her pale midriff bare. She wore a ruffled black and purple skirt that did not come close to reaching the tops of her thighs. But the biggest shock was her shoes. Like Winter, her combat boots were gone, replaced by ballet heels that gave her a solid eight inches of additional height.

Both women gladly accepted their drinks and spent the rest of the evening flirting with some of my regular customers. They very much enjoyed themselves and I was certain everyone enjoyed them as well.

Once Winter and Flame left Blossom House, stories slowly started to make their way back to me. Some were simple stories about the newest two bimbos in Blossom, how they had maintained their goth personas, outside of being complete bimbos, and how they seemed to be every bit of a Blossom House product.

The hotel manager even told me about the noise complaints he got about them bringing a few men back to their room with them. He had been mad at first, but they found it in themselves to make it up to him. They joined he and his wife that night in the manager's apartment for a foursome that the manager very much enjoyed.

They also found themselves apologizing to the neighbors who complained. It seemed they were equally good at eating pussy as they were at sucking cock.

Eventually, however, it was time for Winter and Flame to leave Blossom. They were tourists after all and not permanent residents.

And so it was with some degree of sadness that I instructed Violet give them a drink I had created that would reverse all the changes and turn them back into the goth women they had been before they encountered me and Blossom House. I even had Violet offer them a complete makeover in her salon, making sure they left Blossom exactly how they wanted to.

I never expected to see them again, knowing they had a ferry to catch soon. However, I happened to catch sight of them once more in the book store. Curious, I walked in and browsed in an adjacent aisle, eavesdropping.

"We need to come back here again soon," Winter said.

"I was just thinking that," Flame countered. "This weekend was so much fun. I could definitely see us living here. Could you imagine that?"

"Maybe Asher will join us next time. She could use a break from her cave."

I never did not learn anything more about Asher and her cave, as Winter and Flame moved out of earshot as they moved to the counter to buy whichever books they had selected. I stayed where I was, not wanting to be seen by them.

On their way out of the bookstore, I caught sight of them once more. They looked just as I remembered when I first saw them except for one difference. They each had a pink streak in their hair. Winter let the pink streak fall down the side of her face in a slight change of her previous style. Flame still had her spiky hair, but three of the spikes were now pink.

The pink looked good on them, however, I was wondering if I needed to revisit some of my formulas. They were supposed to be temporary, but clearly something lasted. I could only hope their time in Blossom had opened them to a new way of thinking that they had never considered before, even if they only had vague memories of their time as gimbos.

24

WHY MOVE TO BLOSSOM PART 1

Jake excitedly stood at the bow of the ferry as it pulled into Blossom Harbor. His wife, Mildred, stood beside him, surveying their new home.

"Isn't it beautiful?" Jake said. He not only saw the small tourist town for what it was on the surface, but be knew there was something deeper that he, and hopefully his wife, would come to enjoy.

"Sure, I guess," Mildred answered. "I still don't understand why you had to request a posting here. It wasn't like we needed to leave where we were."

"Come on, honey," Jake pressed. "We should be treating this like an adventure. Just imagine all the fun we can have here. Blossom is practically paradise."

Mildred did not think a small rural town on an island could be paradise. Sure, the island and town were beautiful, but she knew there had to be a catch. Otherwise Blossom would not just be a small town. Regardless, however, Mildred had learned not to argue with her husband about such things. He was the one who worked, after all. She could care for their home wherever they lived.

When Jake and Mildred eventually pulled up to their new home, there was a gathering of people out front. A table had been set up on the front lawn and it was piled high with food.

"I've never seen a welcoming like this before," Jake said as he parked the car in front of the garage. It seemed like the whole neighborhood had come out to welcome them.

"Welcome to Blossom," one of the men said after Jake shut the car door after getting out. "I hope you don't mind that we threw you a welcoming party."

"This is great," Jake said as he helped Mildred out of the car. "It was so nice of you all to do this. I'm Jake and this is my wife, Mildred."

It took several minutes to complete the introductions. There were at least 20 people standing on the front lawn. And as soon as those introductions were complete, it took only moments before Jake and Mildred found themselves split up: Jake with the men and Mildred with the women.

The men immediately welcomed Jake into their fold, treating him like a member of the club. Jake did not know if there was an official club, but the atmosphere was part of what attracted him to Blossom in the first place.

The other major part of what attracted Jake to Blossom were the women. Every single woman who lived in Blossom was hot. He had never seen such a high proportion of attractive women anywhere. And the rumors were the people of Blossom had found some sort of fountain of youth with the way all the women got hot in short order.

Mildred, unfortunately, did not feel herself welcomed to the same degree as her husband had. She knew she was a bit stuffy. She blamed her name, having been named after her grandmother who had passed away just before she was born. Her grandmother was stuffy too. But all of that was really just an excuse for Mildred. After settling into a routine with

Jake, she had let herself stagnate. She found her comfort zone and never liked to test the limits she had placed on herself.

Those limits were being tested by the women she now found herself amongst. It was not just that Mildred did not feel comfortable in most social situations, which she did not. There was something about the women. There was a syrupy sweetness to them all that unnerved her. Not to mention that they all appeared to satisfy nearly every man's dream with their physical attributes.

The one saving grace to the whole ordeal in Mildred's mind was the great layout of food. She was happy to learn it all had come from a local establishment called Blossom House. Apparently all the locals could eat and drink for free. All the services of Blossom House were free to the residents of Blossom.

Mildred had never heard of such a thing, but all the women enthusiastically told her she and Jake needed to visit, now that they too were residents. "It's the best place ever," was one woman's description of the establishment. Not that Mildred had a lot of faith in any of these women's opinions. While they seemed to have won the physical lottery, they all seemed rather lacking when it came to their mental functions. They all seemed more like trophy wives than regular contributors to society.

Eventually the food was eaten and the party was close to breaking up. Before the guests all left, however, the men helped unload the car, taking everything inside. The moving van was still a day away, but Jake and Mildred had packed enough in their car to get them through their first night in Blossom.

Of course, the women simply tittered and cooed as their men did all the work. Even Mildred found herself sitting back and letting her husband direct their unexpected help. After all that food, she felt rather sedate.

That was except for one thing that seemed to get her blood flowing. Maybe it was watching all those attractive men lift and carry her and Jake's possessions inside the house. Or maybe it was seeing Jake take charge, directing said attractive men where to put everything. Either way, Mildred found herself more turned on than she had felt in years, possibly since their honeymoon.

Mildred had never considered what breaking in a new home could mean. But for the first time in her life, she felt as if having sex in their new house was what would most make it a home.

25

WHY MOVE TO BLOSSOM PART 2

It had been three days since Jake and Mildred had first arrived in Blossom. They had spent most of their time unpacking, especially after the movers arrived with their belongings. The rest of their time they spent together.

Mildred did not know what it was, but she felt constantly turned on. It was not just that she was aroused. She had been aroused before. But it seemed like everything she thought about made her think of sex.

When the dining room table and chairs were moved into the house, she could not help but think about how she could use them for sex. She imagined Jake pushing her face first onto the dining room table and taking her from behind.

Mildred would never do something like that, however. She was a proper woman. Sex was meant for the bedroom, or in the case of their first night in their new house, wherever they happened to have set up their sleeping bags for the night.

Despite Mildred's refusal to have sex outside the bedroom, even she had to admit she and Jake were having a lot of sex. More than their honeymoon even. Not that Jake seemed to be complaining. Despite Mildred's reservations about picking up and moving to a little island town like Blossom, it seemed to have done wonders for their marriage. They had never felt closer.

It was on that third day when Jake suggested they have dinner at Blossom House. The neighbors had been nice enough to bring them food each day, wanting to help them get settled in. More than one of the wives, however, admitted they had gotten the food from Blossom House, rather than making it from scratch. The food had been good, so Mildred saw no harm in it.

It was only when Jake and Mildred were welcomed into Blossom House by a scantily clad, and slightly flighty, blonde that Mildred truly began to wonder if they had stepped into an episode of the Twilight Zone.

Mildred had been able to explain away the well endowed women that were their neighbors. They had moved into a nice neighborhood. She was not surprised to see trophy wives. However, with the restaurant at Blossom House nearly full with residents and with the young women working there, it was clear that bra retailers in town made a killing. Every woman in the place was more than twice the size of Mildred. For the first time in her life, Mildred felt inadequate.

The young woman who greeted Jake and Mildred introduced herself as Ella. She wore a short skirt and a top that showed both a generous amount of cleavage and the sparkling belly button piercing in her navel. Her long blonde hair completed the look of the bimbo that she seemed to be.

Once Ella showed the couple to a table, she left them with a giggle, making it clear she put far more effort into her appearance than she did her intelligence.

Despite the preference of the staff to focus on their appearances rather than their intelligence, Mildred enjoyed herself. Her meal was fantastic, possibly the best restaurant meal she had ever had before. And the drinks were even better. She was three cocktails in before she even realized it. Yet despite that fact, she did not feel particularly drunk. More just pleasantly buzzed.

At some point during the meal, the benefactor that made Blossom House possible introduced themselves and explained all of what Blossom House offered. The personal trainer seemed especially appealing to Jake. And despite not being a fan of hard exercise, Mildred found herself agreeing to meet with the trainer by the end of the week. It just seemed like the thing to do in the moment.

After the conversation with the Blossom House benefactor, it seemed as if half the people enjoying Blossom House themselves came to introduce themselves. Mildred quickly became glassy eyed, knowing she would never remember who all these people were. However, she was once again surprised how much the women acted as pretty faces, letting their husbands, boyfriends, and in several cases, fuckbuddies, do all the talking. Had Mildred not been so pleasantly buzzed, she would have balked at such public utterances.

When Jake and Mildred finally returned home that night, the sun was just beginning to set. The couple went out on the back deck to watch it. Jake opened a bottle of wine, a house warming gift from the people of Blossom House.

Normally, Mildred would have ended her drinking at the restaurant. But there was something about the situation where she struggled to say no. Jake wanted to continue drinking and Mildred found herself joining in. And she quickly found, just like at the restaurant, the wine did not so much make her drunk as it did continue the pleasant buzz.

As the sun set, Mildred became aware of something else. She was not just growing aroused, she figured she had to be the most aroused she had ever been. Once the bottle of wine was finished, Mildred found herself sitting on her husband's lap. From there, it was only a few small movements before she was riding him for her first orgasm outside of the bedroom.

Later that night, as Mildred got ready for bed, she realized she had broken her self-imposed rule. She also realized how silly that rule had been. Who cared where she and Jake had sex? Certainly not her anymore.

But it was not until the following morning when Mildred found herself questioning everything. She woke up, feeling surprisingly good considering how much she drank the night before. Mildred padded into the bathroom to start her shower. She pulled off her nightgown and started the water. As she waited for the water to get hot, she took a moment to look at herself in the mirror.

And that was when it struck her. "Honey, are my breasts getting bigger?" she called out.

26

WHY MOVE TO BLOSSOM PART 3

"Honey, are my breasts getting bigger?" Mildred called out from the bathroom. She had been about to hop in the shower when she took a moment to look at herself in the mirror. And to her complete shock, her breasts appeared bigger to her.

Jake came into the bathroom, giving her a look up and down before he answered her question. "Maybe," he said. "You know that's not something I'm good with."

"They look bigger," Mildred said as she reached up and touched them. "And I think they feel bigger too."

"Do you think you're just retaining water?" Jake questioned. "Or maybe it's something hormonal, what with all the sex we've been having."

This time it was Mildred's turn to say, "Maybe." She looked back at her reflection, her face showing a thoughtful look.

"Are you going to shower or not?" Jake asked after a moment.

"Oh, yeah, thanks," Mildred said, shaking her head to clear her thoughts. Yes, her breasts getting bigger was definitely unusual, but there were plenty of reasons for them to swell a little. She decided it would be easiest to just keep a watchful eye on them over the next few days.

As it turned out, however, it did not take long for Mildred to forget to do exactly that. It was not that Mildred did not care about her growth spurt, nor had she stopped noticing it. The simple fact was, Mildred found herself enjoying the results of bigger breasts. She enjoyed the deeper line of cleavage.

But most important, she felt less overshadowed by the other women in town. Mildred had a long way to go before she could rival the less well-endowed women in Blossom, but walking through town it was impossible not to be impressed with all the boob and ass on display. And if anything, such displays only served to turn Mildred on all the more.

There was a second benefit to having larger breasts that did not take Mildred long to appreciate. Sex with Jake seemed even better. His hands would grab and grope her breasts during sex, forcing her arousal all the higher and that only seemed to heighten her orgasms.

By the end of the week, Jake was finally preparing to start at his new office. They had made great headway in unpacking their belongings and making their house livable. However, in Mildred's mind they were far behind schedule.

Of course, she was fully aware of the reason for being behind her schedule. It was the sex breaks. And with her ever growing arousal, those sex breaks only seemed to happen more frequently. They seemed to last longer too.

Not that Mildred was complaining. Sex with her husband was fantastic. It had never been better. And now that she had given up her rule about keeping it in the bedroom, it was as if a whole new sexual world had been opened up to them.

When Friday morning rolled around, Mildred was

looking forward another day of unpacking interspersed with bouts of sex. Mildred planned to finally tackle her book collection, which still remained in boxes. She had meant to do it earlier, but she kept finding excuses to do other things.

However, after a quickie with Jake first thing, he reminded her about her personal training appointment. Mildred groaned at the intrusion into her already planned out day. She had simply forgotten.

Never one to back out of a scheduled appointment, Mildred set herself to getting ready to meet with the Blossom House personal trainer. It seemed strange that a restaurant would also provide all these other services, but clearly it worked for them. And so Mildred went to Blossom House.

Mildred felt awkward walking into Blossom House dressed as she was. The baggy t-shirt and sweatpants were what she had always worked out in, when she worked out. That did not mean she wanted to walk around town dressed as she was. Nor did she want to be seen walking into what she had come to realize was the most popular place on the island dressed as she was.

It was the same girl at the door who greeted her, Ella. She was dressed just as provocatively as she had when Mildred and Jake came for dinner. However, rather than find Mildred a table, Ella directed her to Madison's office.

As Mildred quickly began to find, Blossom House was much more than just a restaurant. And in only a moment, Mildred found herself sitting across from Madison at a small conference table.

Madison was dressed how she always was, wearing a sports bra and a pair of spandex shorts with her white blonde hair tied up in a ponytail. She looked like she would be ready to workout at a moment's notice.

Once the greetings were complete, Mildred found herself

overwhelmed by the fact Madison already had a fitness and nutrition plan for her. It was a variation of the New Arrivals Program. Mildred had no idea what that entailed, but it was only moments longer before Madison was ushering her off to another part of Blossom House.

Mildred did not understand why she needed to visit Violet, the stylist, before her workout, but she did not find it in herself to question. Madison had such a presence that Mildred found it difficult to do anything but agree with her.

As it turned out, Violet answered some of Mildred's unasked questions. Although, Mildred would struggle to remember the answers later. What stuck in her mind was how Madison needed to be able to see her body as she worked out. That mean just working out in a sports bra and small shorts, just like Madison did.

When Mildred wanted to protest, she once again found her voice internally silenced. She was sure the whole program was just a scam to get her to buy stuff from Blossom House. Provide the training for free, but charge heavily for the equipment. But much to her surprise, Violet offered her a new sports bra and shorts set for free. Mildred was no economist, but she certainly knew the value of free.

When Mildred returned to Madison from Violet to the complete her workout, she could not help but feel self-conscious about how she compared to Madison. Her body could not hope to ever match her trainer's.

Their shorts matched though. That was the one takeaway Mildred had. They both wore hot pink spandex shorts, although Madison's were definitely a smaller size, even with having to stretch around her amazing ass. Mildred felt like her shorts just had to stretch around everything.

While their shorts matched, their sports bras did not. Madison wore a bright yellow sports bra that contrasted nicely with her tan skin. Mildred had been given a bright blue sports bra. Again, it was a bigger size than Madison's and it did not look nearly as good, what with Madison's fantastic cleavage. Mildred actually felt jealous.

With all that time taken up, there was not a lot of time for Mildred's first workout, but even that short amount of time left her muscles sore and tired. She left wearing the outfit she had been given while clutching both a nutrition plan and a workout schedule, much of which she could perform at home.

By the time Mildred arrived home, she had forgotten all about her shame of wearing such revealing athletic gear, as well as how she had left her baggy clothes with Violet.

"How did it go?" Jake asked later that day. By then she had changed back into her normal clothes. The workout clothes she had been given had been rinsed out and were now drying on the clothes line in the backyard. Mildred realized she would need to wear them again. And soon, assuming she followed the training plan Madison had given her.

"Good, I think," Mildred answered. "It was kind of over-whelming at first. I didn't even know there was a full gym at Blossom House."

"Isn't it great?" Jake said. "That place has to be the best thing that's ever happened to this town."

"Let's not talk about that," Mildred said, approaching her husband and placing a hand on his chest. "I had a whole day of fun planned and now we have to make up for lost time."

Jake smiled. He was not about to miss Mildred's plans for them. Mildred was smiling too. She was horny and there was only one thing that would fix that. Jake.

27

WHY MOVE TO BLOSSOM PART 4

"Yes, they are definitely bigger," Jake answered. It was another morning and Mildred was once again standing in front of the mirror looking at her naked form. She had once again asked if Jake thought her breasts were bigger.

In Jake's opinion, it was impossible not to see that they were bigger. They had been growing in size ever since they arrived in Blossom, much to his delight. The fact Mildred had to ask him for his opinion would have been comical if he did not have some idea of what she was going through.

And of course, her workout routine and nutrition plan were taking fast effect. Jake had never seen Mildred so slim. And her slimness only further highlighted how much her breasts had grown. Her ass too. It had started to round out nicely. Not that Mildred had seemed to notice.

"Do you think that's okay?" Mildred asked. She had a worried pout on her face. It bordered on confused. Jake thought she looked cute that way. "Like, do you think something might be wrong with me?"

"Do you feel bad?" Jake asked, feigning worry. He was not

worried at all. As far as he could tell, every change he had noticed in his wife was a positive. She was looking better everyday and the sex was fantastic. He could not wait to see what happened to Mildred next.

"Um, no," Mildred said thoughtfully. "Actually, I feel really good. And really horny. Do you think you have time for some fun before work?"

"For you?" Jake said with a smile. "Always."

Without waiting for a response from his wife, Jake picked up his wife and carried her toward their bed. She giggled the entire way, enjoying the feel of her husband's strong body against hers.

He gently tossed her onto the bed. She landed on her hands and knees and quickly assumed a position to give Jake easy access to her pussy.

Mildred generally did not think much about it anymore, but her sex life had changed drastically since she moved to Blossom. All her old rules seemed to have fallen away, usually broken without her even thinking about it. Yes, they still regularly had sex in the bedroom, but it was not the lights off missionary sex that she had always insisted on before.

It was not long before Mildred was practically screaming, begging for Jake to fuck her harder and faster. That had been another significant change in sex for Mildred. She not only had developed a taste for something more rough, but she now vocalized herself so much more.

It was not long after she started begging that she lost the ability to speak coherently at all. With each thrust of her husband's cock, Mildred let out a high pitched moan. She felt like a sex rag doll and she loved it.

As Jake's pace grew erratic, Mildred was vaguely aware that he was getting close. Vague was the only way to describe it, however, because her brain was simply beginning to shut down in response to such overwhelming pleasure.

And when Jake finally pushed into her one last time, holding himself inside of her as he came, shooting hot white cum into her waiting pussy, she came too, her whole body vibrating as wave after wave of orgasmic energy pulsated through her.

When Jake finally pulled out, Mildred was barely conscious. By then her arms had given way and she simply laid there, her ass still sticking up, her head turned to the side, her eyes open, but staring off into nothingness. The lights were on, but no one was home.

By the time Mildred finally shook herself out of her post-orgasm bliss, she discovered Jake had left her. He had to get to work. She understood that, although she wanted nothing more than to have him fuck her brains out for the second time that morning. If she were honest with herself, she would have been ecstatic if that was what the rest of her life consisted of, just getting fucked over and over by her stud of a husband.

The fact Mildred had not always thought of her husband as a stud did not occur to her. She had always loved him, but more and more she was beginning to think how lucky she was for him to have chosen to marry her.

Everyday she saw all the amazingly beautiful and sexy women in Blossom. She felt like she could never compare to them. Yes, her bigger breasts and trimmer waist certainly helped her fit in, but she still felt as if she had an impossible hill to climb if she were ever going to stand beside the other wives of Blossom with pride.

However, Mildred's thoughts about other Blossom women were short lived. Her phone beeped, reminding her of her next training session. She had been diligent for the past week, following Madison's plan for her to the letter.

This time Mildred felt completely normal walking into Blossom House in her workout gear. She certainly recognized the stylishness of her outfit. And despite the changes to her body, losing weight in her less desirable areas, she was surprised how both items continued to fit her. Yes, her breasts were bigger, and so too was her ass, but she lost so much other unneeded weight that they two seemed to compensate for each other. However, as much as Mildred thought she looked good, she knew she would need to get new workout clothes again soon.

Ella greeted Mildred at the door to Blossom House again and waved her straight through to Madison's office. This week Mildred thought nothing of Ella's skimpy attire. Some part of Mildred had grown used to seeing women in town dressed sexily, but she had also started to admire the confidence and sexiness of women like Ella, to show off their bodies with such effortlessness.

Madison was dressed the same as the week before, wearing a bright yellow sports bra that did little to contain her large breasts and hot pink shorts that were so tight it was clear she wore nothing underneath them. She smiled when she saw Mildred step into her office.

"You're making perfect progress," Madison announced after she had Mildred stand and turn around slowly for her. She wanted to get a full view of Mildred's body.

Mildred had blushed at Madison's request, but she followed directions nonetheless. Hearing that she was on track made her beam with pride, however. She liked to hear that her hard work was paying off. Not that she knew what the end result was going to be.

"Today I want to put you through a set of exercises in the gym and then I'm going to send you to Violet again. She has some good ideas for your look that I think you're going to love."

Mildred could not find it in herself to say anything. It was as if Madison was too perfect. Mildred put her up on a pedestal of perfection. Madison had the body that Mildred would never be able to achieve. She simply nodded her consent.

The workout Madison put Mildred through was both harder and easier than the short one from the week prior. It was easier from the standpoint that Mildred felt stronger and fitter than before. Her workout routine at home was really paying off.

But the workout was harder based on the load and duration. Weights were heavier and length spent on each exercise was longer. By the time the workout was over, Mildred was a sweaty mess. She had never worked so hard in her life before. She could only imagine what Madison would have her do the next week.

"Take a shower," Madison commanded at the conclusion of their workout. "Then go see Violet. There are robes in the locker room. After your time with Violet, drop in and see me again before you leave. I'll have your updated training and nutrition plan ready for you."

Again, Mildred simply nodded her consent, however, this time it had more to do with her level of exhaustion than the deference she felt toward the fittest woman in Blossom.

The hot water felt amazing on Mildred's tired muscles. If she had not needed to see Violet, she would have been happy to stand underneath the hot spray for hours, letting the water massage her muscles.

After her shower, Mildred was grateful for the offered robes. She could not stand the idea of putting her sweaty workout clothes back on over her clean skin. The fluffy pink robe felt delicious against her skin too. She wanted nothing more than to curl up on a couch and sip hot cocoa while watching a romantic movie.

Mildred could see that Violet was expecting her the moment she reported to the stylist. She spotted a new outfit for her in the corner, similarly hot pink spandex shorts, but this time paired with a bright green sports bra.

"Madison said you're making perfect progress," Violet said in greeting. "That means we need to start talking about your style."

"It does?" Mildred said, slightly worried. She knew she was in no state to make important decisions.

"Not to worry," Violet said, seemingly sensing Mildred's concern. "This is all part of the plan and I know just what you need."

Mildred was vaguely aware that she should not be putting so much trust in other people. Her style was her own, but it seemed so easy to just let other people take charge. And no one at Blossom House had led her astray so far.

"To start with," Violet continued with a wave of her hand toward the corner, "I've put together your next week's workout outfit. I think you'll find it fits you better than you old one will from now on. That's what progress can mean for you."

Mildred nodded her head, remembering she had left her old outfit in the locker room. She had not thought the fit of her workout clothes was that bad, but she trusted Violet on such matters.

"But we also need to start thinking about your daily style," Violet said. "You're blossoming into a beautiful woman and you need to start thinking about how you want to be shown off."

In the past, Mildred would have flipped out at such a comment. She was no flower to be shown off. She was a strong and independent woman. But more and more, that felt like a facade she was putting on. Her great plans she kept trying to make always seemed to go awry. Her book collection still remained in boxes a week after wanting to unpack them. They were some of the only things that had not been unpacked. And there was part of Mildred that wondered if she should not bother and take a tax donation with them instead.

"What should I do?" Mildred asked.

"For starters, let's get you dressing better. You've got great tits. You should be showing those puppies off more. Cleavage is the name of the game."

Mildred said nothing, but she giggled at the idea of wearing low cut tops. She had once been against such things, but she had a hard time arguing with Violet. She did have great tits, big tits. And they should be shown off.

"And your legs are a great feature. Really, you should be trying to show those off too. Lots of short stuff, dresses, skirts, shorts. And if you need to wear pants, they should be skin tight so everyone can still tell what great legs you have."

Mildred soaked up the new information, promising herself to follow through on every aspect.

"But style is more than just what clothes you wear," Violet explained. "To be stylish, you have to live it. That means your hair, your skin, your makeup, piercings, tattoos, they all have to be coordinated."

"You think I should get a tattoo?" Mildred asked, slightly shocked. She had always been against tattoos. They seemed so trashy to her.

"It's too early to be thinking about all of that, but I was thinking we could make some choices about your hair, skin and makeup."

"That makes sense," Mildred said, although she was not actually positive that it did. She simply could not find it in herself to disagree with Violet.

"And I was thinking you should consider going blonde."

The words washed over Mildred and like a tsunami. She

had always been proud of her naturally dark hair. Even with blonde being a favorite color in Blossom, she had never seen any reason to change. But Violet making that suggestion seemed to change everything. Suddenly the idea of being blonde really appealed to her.

"I'm not talking about making you a platinum blonde like some of the girls out front. Just something lighter than what you have now. We can always change it later."

"Let's do it," Mildred said, deciding it best to agree to having her hair dyed before she had too long to think about it. She did not want to talk herself out of it.

It ended up taking two trips for Mildred to carry everything out to her car. Violet had done more than just color her hair. She had helped her pick out an entirely new wardrobe. Or at least enough clothes to get her through the next week.

There was a little bit of a chill in the air, so Mildred opted to wear a low cut teal green sweater that highlighted her breasts wonderfully. She paired that with a tight pair of black pants that showed off her sleek legs and growing ass to great effect.

Of course, the blonde hair was the biggest change. The wavy style Violet had chosen to put it in kept finding its way into Mildred's face. Each time she was stunned by the color, but secretly loving how stylish it made her feel.

Madison had been supportive of Mildred's new look when Mildred stopped in to pick up her new training plan. And that support was more than enough to ensure her that she was making the right choice.

Once home, Mildred spent the rest of her day preparing for her husband's return from work. She put her new clothes in her closet, bagging the items she planned to never wear again.

But most importantly, Mildred put on the most important part of her surprise. Violet had helped her pick out some sexy lingerie and Mildred could not wait to put it to use.

When Mildred heard Jake pull into the driveway, she hurried toward the door, dropping to her knees, wearing nothing but her green lingerie that did everything possible to highlight her sexuality, including pushing up her tits as if she were presenting them to him.

As the door handle turned, Mildred licked her lips, she was hungry and she knew just how Jake could feed her.

WHY MOVE TO BLOSSOM PART 5

"Oh, that's nice," Jake groaned as he awoke to the delicious sensation of Mildred sucking his cock. It had become a tradition with Mildred waking her husband up every day with a blowjob.

For her part, Mildred loved her morning ritual. She always seemed to wake up a little before Jake needed to rise. That gave her time to make herself presentable, at least for her morning routine.

On this particular day, she woke up and quickly minced into the bathroom so that she could apply her makeup and change into some fun lingerie. Her collection of lace, silk, and leather garments had grown nearly exponentially since she first arrived in Blossom all those months ago. Not that Mildred thought much about her time before Blossom. She did not think much about anything, actually. Her only goal was supporting her husband, pleasing him as best she could.

There was still a part of Mildred that realized she was no longe the smart woman she had once considered herself to be. Quite frankly, outside of the bedroom and the local gossip ring, Mildred had little idea how life worked. She simply did what she was told, either by Jake, or by the lovely people at Blossom House. After all, she was a bimbo like almost all the other women in town. It was only natural for her to submit to the desires of her husband.

Mildred never would have recognized the woman she used to be if she saw a photograph. Her workouts under Madison's tutelage had left her with a body that rightfully represented her bimboness. She had big tits, a large ass, a tiny waist, and even plump lips that made it clear what her best skills were. She had even reached the point in her workouts where she wore the coveted yellow sports bra. That might not have seen like a big deal to many, but it was a signal that she had turned her body into a pinnacle of bimbo delight.

"I'm never going to get tired of that," Jake announced after he came in Mildred's mouth. She swallowed down his cum eagerly, always loving to get a dose of her man's seed.

Mildred simply giggled in response. She beamed with pride knowing she had done her duty as a bimbo wife. She felt completely fulfilled.

"Let's see," Jake continued as he began to turn his mind from the pleasure he had just received to the day ahead of them. Mildred had given up tryin got think for herself. She knew Jake was smarter than her and she voluntarily decided it was best for him to do the thinking for the both of them. "Oh, that's right. We were going to visit the tattoo and piercing parlor. Time to putting the final touches on you."

Jake bopped Mildred on the nose, sending her into another fit of giggles. This had actually been the moment she had been striving toward for weeks, but she had lost track of the time, forgotten that this was the big day. This was the day that she was finally going to be made the perfect bimbo.

The hard work Mildred had put in to reach this point had been tremendous. She had spent hours working out, getting her body in its best bimbo shape. She had spent hours more with the other bimbos in Blossom, learning from them all the things that made them bimbos.

There had never been one moment when Mildred had finally accepted her destiny. It had been much more of a sliding scale. Each visit she made to Blossom House seemed to push her along to the next level. By the time she was openly calling herself a bimbo, it was too late. The damage had been done and there was no coming back from it. The only thing she could do, which she very much wanted, was to keep going to become the best bimbo she could be.

Violet had been a major influence on Mildred's style. Gone were the frumpy sweatshirts and the boring pants she used to wear. If an article of clothing did not help to display her body, she no longer wore it.

At home, that meant lingerie. She had a large enough supply to wear several different lingerie sets per day, changing as needed, without repeating for several weeks.

Out and about, Mildred had found herself preferring thin sundresses with deep necklines and high hems. If someone could not figure out the color of her underwear within a few minutes of seeing her, the dress was either too long or did not show enough of her chest.

Then there were the heels. Regardless of whether Mildred was at home or out on the street, she always wore heels. Gone were the days of her boring flats. She even worked out in a special pair of high-heeled trainers. They were specifically designed for women who could not stand flatfooted. As for Mildred, her heel collection exploded along with her lingerie collection. She had enough heels to never wear the same pair twice in a month, at least. The way her collection kept growing, it would soon be even less often she would need to wear a pair of shoes a second time.

Despite having woken before Jake to start her day,

Mildred still needed at least an hour to change into clothing that was appropriate for her day out with Jake. Lingerie was fine for the house, as was what she called house makeup, but leaving the house required far more preparation to look her bimbo best.

When she finally did step out of the house on Jake's arm, she wore a white sundress with a design of strawberries all over it. The v-neck of the dress was low enough to show off a bit of the lacy pink bra Mildred wore beneath her dress. The amount of cleavage she showed off would have been huge my most standards, but in Blossom, it was just slightly above average. The shortness of the dress, however, meant it would only take a gust of wind or Mildred bending over for everyone to see that she wore a matching pink thong. With it being a warm summer day, Mildred had opted to wear cork wedge heels with white straps that wrapped over her foot and around her ankle.

Blossom was a small enough town where walking was often the easiest way to get around. Yes, trips to the grocery store often required a car, but as long as one did not mind the hills, walking was the preferred method of transportation whenever possible. This day was no exception as Jake and Mildred made their way to the tattoo and piercing parlor for their scheduled appointment.

"Hi there," the woman behind the counter said as soon as Jake and Mildred stepped inside the shop. She wore a big brainless smile, which made sense, since she was a bimbo, as were almost all the women in Blossom. The only women who were spared the bimbofying effects of Blossom were the tourists. All the residents eventually came under the bimbo spell.

"We have an appointment," Jake said, taking charge.

Men in Blossom had long ago learned the importance of taking charge. If they did not, then they would get nowhere.

After all, with all the women as bimbos, they certainly were not going to be leading the way.

The women looked down at the appointment book sitting open on the counter. She squinted her eyes as she scanned the page, doing her best to read. She still could read, but she generally avoided it, like most bimbos.

Mildred herself had been an avid reader once. However, after arriving in Blossom, she found her interest in the written word waning. She never did unpack the boxes of books she had brought with her. Jake eventually cleared them away, knowing Mildred would not be reading them anymore. If she noticed, she did not say anything. It was just one less thing to risk tripping over as her body grew big tits and her choice in footwear left her never knowing where her feet were going to land.

"Jake and Mildred," Jake said, helping the woman.

There had been a time early in his stay in Blossom that Jake began to wonder if he had made the right decision in uprooting he and Mildred and moving them here. He certainly loved looking at all the bimbos in town and he loved how Mildred was changing. However, he found himself growing hot under the collar when dealing with some of the bimbos around town, growing impatient as they struggled to do their jobs.

Eventually, however, Jake grew used to the change in pace. Some of it came from learning island time, which always seemed to be a little later and a little slower than expected. There was also bimbo time, which was like island time, but to a greater extreme. It also helped that all the sex with Mildred kept his mood in check. The truth was, he needed the sex as much as she did.

"Oh, yeah, here you are," the woman finally said, crossing out the name in the appointment book with a pink gel pen. "My name's Olivia and I'll be your artist and piercer today."

Olivia was decked out almost head to toe in tattoos and piercings. She had kept her face and neck clear of tattoos, but the rest of her body was heavily decorated with both arms done up in full sleeve tattoos, as well as several on the exposed portions of her chest, belly and back. The piercing work was by no means extreme, but she sported several less common piercings, in addition to the usual suspects.

Despite Olivia's bimbo qualities, when it came to her work, she was meticulous and on top of her game. It only took a little discussion about what Jake had planned for his wife before she invited them both back into the more secluded work room. Mildred said nothing. She did not need to. Everyone knew who was in charge and as a bimbo wife, she had already given up her autonomy to her husband. If he wanted her to get tattoos or piercings, she would. There was no question about it.

The work being done was actually quite simple. First up was the piercing work. Mildred already had her ears pierced, but Jake wanted her tongue pierced too. He loved getting blowjobs from his wife, but he knew they could be improved with a little metal in her mouth. Yes, she might end up with a lisp, but there was not much that Mildred ever said that mattered. They both knew the blowjobs were more impor-tant than anything a bimbo like her had to say.

Once that was complete, Olivia pulled out the tattoo materials. She started by drawing on the insides of both of Mildred's wrists. Olivia's previous artistic skills still coming into use. And once Jake approved of the hand drawn designs, the real work began.

When Jake and his bimbo left Blossom Tattoo that day, they both knew Mildred's transformation was complete. On her left wrist were the words Jake's Bimbo in two small lines of script. On her right wrist was the word Millie. That was her bimbo name and the only name she would ever use again. And if she ever forgot, which as a bimbo was not out of the realm of possibility, it would alway be there on her right wrist. And if she ever forgot who she was, she would only have to look down on her left wrist to know that she was Jake's bimbo.

The reasons for moving to a small town can be many, but the reasons for moving to Blossom are much simpler. Yes, Jake knew all along what would happen to his wife when they moved to Blossom. He had planned for this. But little did he understand that moving to Blossom did not just make himself happier. It made his wife happier as well. And as a bimbo, Millie could not imagine a better life than the one she shared with Jake in Blossom.

MOVING ON FROM BLOSSOM

When making my move to Blossom, I followed a grand plan. By creating Blossom House, I used my money and resources to add to the already thriving community present. Yes, I came here to bimbofy the town, but something more happened during my stay. I fell in love with Blossom.

And it is because of that love that I find this moment bittersweet. It will be time for me to move on.

Bimbofying a town like Blossom is a perfect use of my skills. And it is certainly fun. I thoroughly enjoyed myself for these past few years.

However, at this point, the town is virtually self-sustaining. It no longer needs me pulling my strings to function. For those women who move here, they will find themselves on the path toward bimbodom on their own. For those women who come of age in Blossom, they will already be on their own path to be bimbos just like their mothers, their friends, their role models. I am no longer needed.

It was a beautiful summer day as I waited for the ferry to arrive to carry me away. I had stopped in the ice cream shop by the harbor. Shaniqua was there offering scoops as she had since I first bimbofied her. Both she and the other two bimbos working behind the counter simply wore bikinis now, their nipples perpetually hard from frequently leaning over into the freezer as they scooped out the ice cream.

I casually licked my chocolate fudge ice cream on a sugar cone, my usual order as I sat on a bench overlooking the harbor.

I had already said good-bye to my girls. They each held a soft spot in my heart and I knew I would never forget them, whether it was Ella and her determination to be the head bimbo of Blossom House or it was Zella who liked to act like the bad girl before she dropped to her knees to suck cock. Then there was Violet who needed a little extra guidance to finally break out of her seriousness and reach her bimbo potential. And all the others as well. I would always remember them and the work we did here.

"Hey there, stranger," said a man as he sat down next to me on the bench. "Who'd have figured I would run into you here?"

I looked up from my ice cream to find an old friend sitting beside me.

"Dr. Scott," I said. "What drags you all the way up here? Taking a break from the Bimbo Ward in Los Angeles?"

Dr. Scott was not exactly a friend. He was more of a colleague. He had tried to recruit me to come work at the Bimbo Ward once, but I had passed, preferring to work along. Still, we saw each other at various conferences and events from time to time. Although Blossom had taken up much of my attention for the past several years. I had hardly left the island in that span.

"I heard there was a perfect bimbo town up here and I just had to check it out for myself," Dr. Scott said. "To be honest, I thought it sounded like your work, but I had figured you had retired by now. I haven't seen you at the annual conference for a couple years."

I shrugged my shoulders as I continued to eat my ice cream.

"I've had other things to do," I finally said.

"I can see that," Dr. Scott said. "This place is amazing. I don't know how you've gotten away with it."

"I had a few close calls," I admitted. "There have been a few reporters snooping around, but I took care of them."

Dr. Scott wolf whistled as a bimbo walked by in a short skirt that hugged her ass and a cropped top that showed both a generous amount of cleavage, as well as a sizable amount of under boob. Her whole body was a marvel of bimbo proportions. She turned her head and blew Dr. Scott a kiss with her thick lips.

"Who's that?" Dr. Scott asked.

"I honestly don't know," I answered truthfully.

When I started, I completely had my pulse on the town, knowing almost everybody. But over the years, more people had fallen into my net and I lost the ability to keep track of them all. I didn't mind. That was a big part of my plan. But when it became clear that I no longer needed to control the town, that it held a life of its own, I knew it was time to move on. This woman was just another example of it.

"You have any trouble with reversion?" Dr. Scott asked. "With this big a population, even though it's a small town, you must have had somebody break the mold."

"Just one," I said, pointing toward an old political poster in a shop window across the street. "Mayor Dani reverted on me. She was the only one. I figured it out in the end. And even though she's just a figurehead now and her husband is running the show from behind the scenes, she still won the last election, garnering every vote. And the election wasn't even rigged for her. Those were the honest results. Her opponent was her husband. He figured he might as well get the credit for the work he was putting in. But the people wanted Dani."

Dr. Scott laughed. "That's hilarious. But seriously, you've really done something amazing here. I wouldn't have believed it all if I hadn't seen it with my own eyes."

For the first time I felt as if I had really accomplished something in Blossom. Hearing Dr. Scott, a man I respected, praise my work was something I hadn't expected. I honestly did not know what to say.

"Thank you," I finally choked out, feeling as if my eyes might start tearing up at any moment.

"What's next for you?" Dr. Scott asked. "From the looks of it, you could just retire right here and enjoy the rest of your days."

"I could do that," I said. To be honest, I had considered staying. I was a respected member of the community. I could let my roots really settle and just enjoy my life from here on out. But that wasn't my style. I was a bimbofier at heart. If I wasn't turning people into bimbos, it would feel like I wasn't myself. But staying would also attract danger. Dr. Scott had found me and he wasn't even trying. There were dangerous forces at work in the world. Bimbofiers like me, who worked on our own, had to be careful.

"But you won't," Dr. Scott said. "I understand. I honestly don't know if I'll ever be able to retire. The draw is just too big."

"Agreed."

"So where will you go?"

I looked to my colleague sitting beside me, giving him a questioning look.

"I'm sorry," Dr. Scott said. "That's none of my business. You have to keep some things close to the chest. I get it. It's different for me at the Bimbo Ward. The money we produce and get from the foundation protects us. You don't have that luxury. Still, I don't know how you'll ever top this. Blossom is a bimbo masterpiece."

I was about to speak, but the ferry sailed into view. In a few minutes it would dock and begin to unload its passengers. Then it would be my turn to board.

"That's my ferry," I said.

"And you better be on it," Dr. Scott agreed. "But before you go…"

I smiled, reaching into my pocket with my ice cream free hand and pulled out a card. I had several of these, all with the names of my girls, how to reach them, and what their specialties were.

"Enjoy yourself," I said, handing the card to Dr. Scott.

We two bimbofiers went our separate ways. I walked toward the ferry landing, still eating the last of my ice cream cone. Dr. Scott headed up the hill toward Blossom House to fulfill whatever sexual needs he had. I didn't want to know.

It was bittersweet to be leaving, but it was time. Blossom would always hold a place in my heart, but I needed to keep moving. There were other Blossoms that needed to be bimbofied. I already had several leads. It was only a matter of time before I started up again. After all, who was I if I wasn't turning people into bimbos? I never wanted to find out. Maybe I'll see you around. But if you see me, it is safe to assume that I am already at work, bimbofying your town.

ABOUT THE AUTHOR

Sadie Thatcher is a longtime author of erotic fiction, especially related to transformations and bimbofication. She likes to say "I have thrown off the shackles of my conservative upbringing and now write erotic stories."

She maintains several blogs devoted to her writings, including a behind the scenes look at her writing process, and bimbos in general, as well as highlights works by other authors. They can be found at:

https://authorsadiethatcher.tumblr.com
https://buildingbettergiggles.tumblr.com

Acting the Part

Subliminal Society

Inheritance

Company Morale

His Bimbo Girlfriend

The Bimbo Room

The Curse of Playing Bimbo Tag

The Curse of Playing Bimbo Tag: Jenna or Jenni

The Bimbo Professor: The Curse of Playing Bimbo Tag Book 3

Anything for the Job

Anything for the Job 2

Anything for His Job

The Bimbo in the Mirror

The Bimbo in the Mirror 2

Astrid and the Bimbo Bee

Bella and the Bimbo Bee

Cali and the Bimbo Bee

Bimbo Halloween

Bimbo Christmas

Bimbo Technology

Dorm Room Bimbo

Carissa's Magic Pen

Spirit Walk

Muscle Memory

The Case of the Bimbo Wife

Changes

Changes 2

New Year New You

The Bimbo Dream

The Wedding Gift

The Cure

Backfire

Bim & Bo Yoga

Wishing for Each Other

Bimbo Roots

Body Swap Rings: Happy Anniversary

Body Swap Rings 2: Wedding Night

The Bimbo Experience

The Bimbo Experience 2

The Bimbo Experience 3some

The 4th Bimbo Experience

Bimbo Genes

Bimbo Genes II: The Virus

The Bimbo Genes III: The Epidemic

Bimbo Juice: Blue Raspberry

Bimbo Juice: Grape

Bimbo Juice: Mango

Bimbo Juice: Pineapple

Bimbo Juice: Red Apple

Bimbo Juice: Veggie

Bimbo Juice Gone Wild: The Muse

Bimbo Juice Gone Wild: Street Racer

Bimbo Juice Gone Wild: Score

Bimbos of the Traveling Earrings: Book 1

Bimbos of the Traveling Earrings: Book 2

Bimbos of the Traveling Earrings: Book 3

Bimbos of the Traveling Earrings: Book 4

Bimbo Party: Kennedy

Bimbo Party: Esme

Bimbo Party: Ariana

Bimbo Party: Tara

Workout Buddies

Wishful Thinking

Wanting More

Bimbo Harem: Annabelle

Bimbo Harem: Josie